COMPROMISING WILLA

Other books by Diana Quincy

COMPROMISING WILLA

THE ACCIDENTAL PEERS SERIES

DIANA QUINCY

Entangled Publishing, LLC
2614 South Timberline Road
Suite 109
Fort Collins, CO 80525
Visit our website at www.entangledpublishing.com.

Edited by Kate Fall and Alethea Spiridon Hopson
Cover design by Heidi Stryker

Manufactured in the United States of America

Ebook ISBN 978-1-62266-414-0

First Edition December 2013

To Megann

For being the first person to talk about my characters as though they were real people, and for her fierce devotion to these characters in particular.

Chapter One

Augustus Manning sat by the sickbed, waiting for his father to die. The air was humid with the rancid scents of illness and impending death. Closed velvet curtains rebuffed the afternoon light, cloaking the chamber in long shadows. Sunshine had no business in this lifeless place.

The Earl of Bellingham's labored breathing punctured the silence. He sucked in gasping breaths, as though determined to fight off the inevitable for as long as possible. Stubborn to the end. Augustus suppressed an impatient sigh. How much longer would the old man hold on?

He'd waited four interminable years for the bastard's heart to give out. Silence rang through the chamber, and it took him a moment to realize the gasping sounds had ceased. Anticipation stirred in his chest as the doctor leaned over the frail form on the bed before straightening and bowing to Augustus, murmuring words of sympathy.

Suppressing a delighted smile, Augustus rose and drew

back his shoulders, his chest expanding to fill the role to which he'd been born. He strode from the chamber, passing his younger brother, who dragged heavy hands down his ashen face, and his father's faithful valet, who bowed with deference to the new Earl of Bellingham.

The staff, who watched him hurry to the stables before rearing off on his thoroughbred, likely thought pain and anguish drove the dead man's eldest son. But in truth, sheer exhilaration—bright and joyous—broke free inside of him. He would finally have it all: the money, the title, and the lady who inhabited his dreams. The new Earl of Bellingham finally meant to claim what was his.

And nothing and no one was going to stop him.

• • •

Swallowing her nerves, Lady Wilhelmina Stanhope stood to the side of the crowded assembly room and hoped no one took notice of her. Unfortunately, it didn't appear to be working.

Her new friend, Lady Florinda Bromley, threaded through the throng to Willa's side. "You have an admirer. Viscount Mowbry said you are a diamond of the first whose loveliness easily outshines everyone else present this evening."

Willa had already noted Mowbry's interest. The viscount, elegant in evening finery, stood next to a slight fellow in bright colors, sliding an aloof gaze over her with obvious appreciation. She pretended not to notice the polite inspection, comprehending full well that nothing would come of it. At three-and-twenty, she'd never had a proper marriage offer. Except for that one time four years ago. If one could credit that debacle. "Nonsense, Flor, he could be looking at anyone."

"No, I have excellent hearing. He was discussing you with that fop standing next to him." Flor, a slight girl with red curly hair, pushed her spectacles up the bridge of her nose with her pointer finger. "After all, who else present is in possession of chocolate-colored curls of silk and skin like a fine cream?"

"He said that?"

Flor nodded, her green eyes sparkling with wicked humor. "He's not exactly Byron, is he? And I heard him utter the most scandalous thing."

Her stomach lurched. "Scandalous?" She'd had enough scandal to last her a lifetime.

"He said something about large velvet brown eyes and a sumptuous form that made a man think of things he shouldn't when looking at a lady." Amusement lined her forehead. "It would all be enormously flattering if only the viscount weren't a buffoon with nothing but air between his ears."

"Florinda!" Willa couldn't help but smile at the girl's audacity. They'd become fast friends this season—her new cohort's blunt nature being one of the qualities she admired most. It helped that the earl's daughter knew everything there was to know about Town, unlike Willa, whose parents had always preferred country living.

"Look, he's coming towards us." Flor's skeptical gaze followed the viscount. "I'd wager he'll ask someone for an introduction."

Apprehension rolled in her stomach. She darted a look

at the gentleman, who did indeed appear to be heading in their direction. He was waylaid by his companion, a well-known dandy and gossip, who put a staying hand on his lordship's arm and murmured something into his ear. The viscount's eyebrows inched up a little at a time as he listened, then his gaze darted back to Willa. Only this time, the bold appraisal lacked any pretense of courtesy, wandering over her curves with insolent scrutiny, as though he could see straight through her gown.

"The blackguard!" Flor inhaled a shocked breath. "Did you see the discourteous manner in which he regarded you?"

Willa's gut twisted. The way he'd looked at her made her feel like a strumpet. It intensified the uneasy feeling which had lingered all evening. The curious glances from some guests, the whispers when she passed one group of matrons. Clearly, rumors of her ruination still circulated. One would think there'd be a new scandal for the *ton* to focus on by now.

Ignoring her discomfort, she slipped her arm through Flor's. "Come now. I, for one, intend to enjoy this evening. It is my first Season in years."

She surveyed the dancing couples and groups of people sitting or standing at the edges of the hall against crimson wallpaper and carved flattened columns which glimmered under immense two-tiered chandeliers. The chattering crowd grew louder and the air more still with each new arrival. Her sister Addie's come-out ball was proving a great success. There was even talk the Regent himself might make an appearance.

It had been an age since she'd circulated among these people. At first, the threat of scandal had kept her family away after Willa's first and only season. Then her father had fallen ill, lingering for months before succumbing, which led to another year of mourning and seclusion in the country.

"Willa," Flor said as they made their way to the refreshment table. "Perhaps I shouldn't mention this but—"

"Come now, you've never held your tongue before." She squeezed her friend's arm. "Surely you don't mean to start now. I would be sorely disappointed if you did."

Flor gave a grim smile of acknowledgement. "I don't want to upset you, but you shouldn't be taken by surprise."

"Out with it then."

"Augustus Manning is here."

"Augustus?" A sharp pain knifed through her. She'd confided a bit about Augustus to her new friend. Not all of it, of course. She'd never tell anyone the entire truth. "How do you know?"

"I saw him with my own eyes just a few minutes ago. He was heading to the cards room."

"How is that possible? He did not receive an invitation." She darted a look toward the chamber in question, scanning the crowd for the man she had expected to spend a lifetime with, who had instead became the source of her greatest humiliation. "Are you certain it was he?"

Flor nodded, sighing with obvious appreciation. "It is difficult to mistake a gentleman with looks as fine as that."

Her throat felt as though someone had lodged their fist in it. "I suppose it had to happen at some point."

Sympathy lit Flor's eyes. "Come now, forget about that fribble. Let us walk and dazzle everyone with our superior beauty and charm."

"I seem to have torn my gown during the last set," she

lied, eager for escape. "I must have it attended to."

Once free of her friend, she headed to the terrace. To her relief, the long, narrow structure appeared mostly empty. She took a moment to enjoy her reprieve in the quiet coolness of the darkened veranda. Breathing in the clear night air, she tilted her face upward to feel the soft spring breeze brush across her skin.

Augustus. She understood now that it hadn't been a love match, but they had been friends once. Or so she'd thought. The memories flooded back. The two of them, along with his brother and her sister, had spent countless easy summer days as children exploring the grounds surrounding their adjoining estates. And then the inn had happened.

"I see the years have only added to the lady's beauty."

A chill shot up her back as the smooth timbre of Augustus' voice washed over her. Forcing her leaden legs to move, she turned to face him, the dark specter from her past silhouetted by the brilliance of the ballroom behind him.

He'd always been handsome, and the passage of years had ripened that boyish promise into true masculine beauty. Augustus carried his impressive height and long limbs with a lanky, almost careless elegance that spoke of prominent birth and a sense of entitlement. Perfectly ruffled golden hair highlighted a strong jaw that belied the weak man Willa now knew him to be.

"Augustus."

"I see you remain the loveliest rose in all England."

It was a lie of course. She was no great beauty. Her eyes were too big, her lips so large they were almost vulgar, and her figure far more womanly than the preferred current style.

"I heard of your father's passing," he said. "My sincerest condolences, my dearest Willa." He used her nickname casually, as though they still belonged to each other.

"Why are you here? You were not invited."

"An unintended oversight, I'm sure. No matter. For a bit of coin, invitations can be easily redirected."

"You shouldn't have come."

He frowned over the bridge of a nose so straight and symmetrical even Michelangelo would have marveled over it. "Come, Willa, 'tis me, Augustus. What is with such coldness for an admirer who desires nothing more than the precious gift of a lady's smile?"

A kernel of anger stirred inside her. She might appear to be the same naïve girl on the outside, but Willa viewed life through different eyes now, knowing it could change in an instant. She'd learned firsthand, after the disaster with Augustus and then her father's death. The young girl who had challenged Augustus to race their horses through the countryside, her untamed hair flying—jesting with him on the rare occasion that she actually beat him—had vanished. Those summers, and the world of innocent possibility that came with them, seemed like a lifetime ago. "There was a time you asked for far more than a mere smile."

"Let's not dwell on the past," he said. "Not when we have the brightest of futures to look forward to."

"A future?"

"Of course, with the depth of feeling that you and I can only find in each other."

Her throat constricted. "The time for any sort of romantic foolishness has passed." She turned away and rested her gloved hands on the cold stone balustrade, the chill stealing up her arms and rippling through her insides. "Surely, you recognize the realities of the world. You certainly assured that I did."

"Balderdash." He moved beside her, close enough for his perfume to fill her nostrils with the smell of rosemary, almonds, and old memories that were best forgotten. "I have come to take you to wife. Nothing stands between us now."

Her heart took a slight leap. Perhaps she'd been wrong about him. Maybe his regard for her would prove strong enough after all. "The earl has agreed to this?" she ventured, feeling the tiniest sprig of hope. "Or have you decided to proceed without your father's consent?"

He laughed, but it was a mirthless sound. "It is what the Earl of Bellingham desires above all else."

"I don't understand." The old earl had always been firmly opposed to any match between them. He'd been in search of a larger dowry, but Augustus had convinced her they could overcome his objections. Foolishly—disastrously—she'd believed him. "How could this be?"

"My father is dead. Not three days in the ground, and I have come for you because I couldn't bear to wait one moment longer for us to be together." He resumed his smiling demeanor, yet no warmth emanated from him. "Once an appropriate mourning period is past, we shall become betrothed, just as we should have in earnest four years ago."

It took her a moment to comprehend his words. His father dead. After all these years, nothing stood between them. She paused, waiting for a warm surge of joy now that they could finally be together. But there was...nothing. The only warmth she felt came from the anger kindling in her chest.

"I see." Comprehension sank in. "Do you dare delude yourself into thinking I would accept you now? After the humiliation you inflicted upon me, sir?"

She stilled at the sound of laughter from a couple approaching from the far side of the terrace. She drew back into the shadows, away from Augustus. She had no desire to be seen alone with him and risk resurrecting the old rumors. "Please, take your leave of me. I am not so foolish as to repeat the follies of my past."

He stepped closer. "You are even lovelier in your anger." A satisfied smile crossed his face. "It appears you have grown up, my wild Willa."

"Indeed. I am a great deal wiser than the foolish girl you knew."

"And a great deal more beautiful." He looked at her from under heavy eyelids. "I dare say the secret pleasures of marriage will be even more enjoyable than I've anticipated all these years."

Her stomach revolted at the thought of resuming any kind of intimacy with this man. "I shall never marry."

"Now, now. That will never do. Surely you comprehend that a female who displeases God by refusing to take a husband and procreate is consigned to lead the apes into hell."

"I would much prefer to guide the monkeys into Hades rather than become your wife."

"You, an ape leader? Such loveliness would be wasted on the shelf." Cool eyes skated over the curves of her body. "I would enjoy pressing the issue, but it won't do for my future countess to be tainted by further scandal."

She gritted her teeth. "I will never marry. Not you nor anyone else."

"Nonsense." He drew back and executed a quick bow. "We are meant to be together. No one else shall ever have you." Spinning on his heels, he marched into the ballroom.

She squelched the urge to fling something hard and heavy at the earl's retreating back. Furious thoughts crowded her head. How had she ever borne such a disagreeable man? To have contemplated a life with him?

Only a foolish young girl would have considered it. Her own come-out Season years ago had met with great success, but she'd only had eyes for Augustus, who'd pressed his suit despite his father's vehement disapproval. It shamed her to wonder whether his undeniable good looks had swayed her judgment of his character, even after he'd begun to change from the solemn boy she'd befriended into the intolerable man he was now.

A sudden movement at the bottom of the terrace steps cut into her thoughts. The gravel crunched and then went silent.

Someone was down there.

Chapter Two

Willa peered down into the shadows where the light of a garden torch illuminated a masculine face etched in hard lines. He leaned into the flame, giving the unlit cheroot in his mouth a few quick inhales, cajoling it to take. When it sparked and smoked, the man leaned back with a satisfied air, taking a deep inhale.

He was likely a footman staying out of view while taking a break from his duties. Disconcerted, she called out in a chastising tone. "You there, what do you mean by hiding in the shadows listening to private discourse?"

"That was quite a scene," the shadow drawled. "I look forward with great anticipation to seeing how this charming love story concludes." Tall and darkly clothed, his bearing was not that of a servant, but someone of breeding would never smoke in front of a lady.

"You are very insolent," she said heatedly, "to speak to me in such a manner."

He regarded her with amused curiosity. "A thousand pardons, ma'am."

She moved down the stairs to get a better look at him. Closer inspection revealed he wore formal evening attire topped with a snowy cravat. Not a servant then. He took a deep drag and exhaled. Lazy circles of silvery smoke melted into nothingness around the glow of the flame, steeping the air with the pungent aroma of burning tobacco.

"Forgive me if I have transgressed." He stepped away from the torch, the glowing tip of the cheroot dancing in the dark as he moved. "However, in my defense, I was here previous to your romantic assignation on the terrace."

"Romantic assignation? It was no such thing!" She prayed he'd have the good manners to vanish as quickly and quietly as he had appeared.

Instead, the scoundrel chuckled. "Once the heart-warming declarations of love and marriage began, I was keen to learn how it would all resolve itself."

She batted the smoke away in quick, jerky movements. "It was private—"

"Most assignations are," he interrupted, his eyes dancing. "Are felicitations on your impending betrothal in order? Allow me to be the first to bestow them."

"You are insufferable." Embarrassed indignation filled her chest. "A gentleman would have made his presence known. But you are obviously no gentleman."

"So some have said." He drew on his cheroot and exhaled, watching darkness swallow the curling fog of silvery smoke. "But enough about that. Do tell, are you and old Gus stepping into the parson's mousetrap?"

As her eyes adjusted to the lack of light, she could make

out the unforgiving angles of his face. Sharp cut lines which would look quite menacing, if not for the roguish glint in his eyes. "Even if it were so, I surely wouldn't share information of a personal nature with a stranger," she said, her nerves on end. "I do not know you, sir."

"Quite right. I'm suitably chastened." His answering grin flashed white in the darkness. "Do accept my most humble apologies." His hand whipped out to grab her arm. Startled, she jumped back with a cry of alarm. His ungloved fingers tightened around the bare skin of her arm above her silk evening gloves, and the shock of flesh on flesh sizzled through her.

"What are you doing?" she hissed, struggling as he dragged her behind the hedgerow. Jerking his head in the direction of the stairs, he brought a long finger to the firm curve of his lips, signaling for her to be silent. She followed his gaze to the top of the stairs, where a couple prepared to descend. She clamped her mouth shut. The last thing she needed was another hint of scandal if she were discovered alone in the garden with a strange man. Why did she always seem to land herself into these situations?

The glowing tip of the cheroot sailed to the ground, the stranger's boot heel silently coming down to crush the life out of it. They stood frozen while the couple walked down the stairs chatting, passing Willa and the stranger, who remained hidden by the greenery.

The man's tall form stood so near that his body heat lapped at her. He smelled intoxicatingly fresh, like soap, as though he'd just scrubbed himself clean, intermingled with the distinctive scent of tobacco. A heightened sense of her own physicality zipped through Willa; her breathing sounded unnaturally loud; the rhythm of her heart clanged a clumsy beat and her skin warmed despite the evening chill.

"Please unhand me, sir." Disconcerted by her peculiar bodily reaction to him, she shrugged his hand off the moment the couple moved out of earshot.

"What was it you mentioned to your amorous suitor? Something about the follies of your past? I took it upon myself to spare you any further embarrassment."

Beastly man. Inside, she churned with humiliation, but on the outside, her face assumed the cool, imperious cloak it wore so well. The one that kept people at bay.

"Surely I deserve words of praise from the lady," he continued, "rather than her scorn?"

"Alas," she said tartly, "the words you truly deserve would never pass a lady's lips."

Perfecting her posture, she turned away. Taking pains to appear unhurried, she sailed back up the stairs while his quiet laughter drifted behind her in the darkness.

• • •

The Earl of Bellingham sipped watery lemonade while watching a pretty brown-haired maid set more of the tepid liquid out in the refreshment room. So Willa planned to resist him. He went hard just thinking about it. She'd been damned appealing back when she'd been willing. But now, all fiery and reluctant, she was spectacular. Once the chit belonged to him, he'd enjoy bringing her back into submission.

The clatter of glasses turned his thoughts back to the brown-eyed maid and the sway of her generous hips. He quietly followed the wench along the narrow service corridor until they were alone in a tight alcove between the main assembly rooms and the kitchen.

"Girl," he called out.

She stopped at once and turned around. The usual appreciation his physical appearance drew from wenches flickered in her widening eyes. "May I be of service, my lord?"

The light slanted across her unremarkable features, revealing the girl to be rather plain of face. No matter, he needed relief and she would do well enough. Advancing on her, he flicked a coin in her direction. It clattered to the ground before she could think to catch it. "Yes, you could be of service to me."

She looked confused for a moment until her gaze fluttered down to his obvious arousal, which he made no attempt to hide. She reddened and backed away, crossing her arms against her chest. "Oh, no my lord. I am a good girl. I could send Stella to ye maybe." Her color deepened. "She'll give ye a toss for a price."

The idea of a willing whore bored him. "No, I'll have you." The fear in her eyes made him harden even more. "Or I shall be forced to let everyone know that you stole that blunt from me."

Eyeing the shiny sovereign winking up at her from the floor, she trembled. "But I didn't, my lord."

"Who do you think they will believe, a peer of the realm or an inconsequential nothing like you?"

She bowed her head as tears filled her eyes. Tasting victory, Augustus' pulse accelerated. His arousal swelled and ached with anticipation.

"Do not concern yourself overmuch. I am not interested

in what's between your legs." He moved in on her, unfastening his breeches. "Get down on your knees, my pet."

• • •

"There you are, Willa." Her cousin, Arthur Stanhope, Marquess of Camryn, stood with her mother. "I believe you owe me a dance."

"We were looking for you," Mother said. "Where did you take yourself off to?"

She smoothed her face, anxious not to appear unnerved. "I stepped out for some air." Her eyes scanned the crowd for any sign of either Augustus or the annoying man from the garden.

"Unaccompanied?" Her mother frowned. "Really, Willa."

Her cousin saved her from further scrutiny by reminding her of their dance. "Now that you are quite refreshed, shall we?" He offered his arm.

"But this is a waltz," Willa teased. "Think of all the maidens you'll disappoint by standing up with your cousin."

"Exactly," he said, leading her out onto the dance floor. "You are the safest option for an unmarried marquess."

Her good-natured cousin made her feel safe as well. The eldest son of her father's brother, Cam had assumed the role of protective older brother after inheriting her father's title. Looking up into his speckled green eyes and at his unruly tawny hair made her smile. Cam had the appearance of an untamed animal in his stiff evening clothes. "Surely you aren't shirking your duty to marry and beget an heir."

"Perhaps it is time for both of us to contemplate the

matrimonial state."

"With my reputation?" She forced a light tone, which belied the heaviness in her chest. "We have been over this more times than I care to count."

"I could arrange an excellent match," he said in a grave tone. "There are many fine gentlemen who would treat you well."

"Thanks to the fortune you'll bestow upon him for accepting me as his wife? No, I am quite happily on the shelf." She lifted her chin. "Now, will you find me a tutor? You did promise."

"You are a peculiar female, cousin." His grave countenance fell away, restoring his usual easy amiability. "Most maidens are interested in the latest fashions rather than world politics and the inner workings of Parliament."

"There's just so much to learn and I've been rusticating in the country for far too long."

"Not to worry. I've already had my man of business inquire into it. It shouldn't be long before he finds a suitable tutor."

Excited by the prospect, Willa favored her cousin with a dazzling smile. Deciding not to marry had freed her to pursue her interests. After the tranquility of country life, she anxiously soaked up London's bustling atmosphere. The metropolis was so alive and dynamic, teeming with remarkable people and new ideas she longed to explore.

She wasn't the same sheltered girl who'd almost become Augustus' wife. Marriage struck her as so limiting now, what with so much of the world waiting to reveal itself. The Ladies Reading Society that Flor had recently introduced her to promised far more excitement than any man could.

Although her mother would suffer the vapors if she learned they were currently reading *The Vindication of the Rights of Women* by Mary Wollstonecraft, whose radical assertion that females were not inferior to males was considered scandalous.

Besides, she'd be a fool to take a husband. With her reputation, only fortune hunters would want her now. Augustus had certainly demonstrated how distasteful the physical side of marriage could be, and her late father's flagrant philandering was a testament to a husband's inconstancy. Except for Cam and his brothers, men were not to be trusted. She'd learned that lesson well. When the music ended, Cam returned Willa to her mother before wandering off to fetch lemonade for the ladies.

"Adela is enjoying herself," Mother said. "Her dance card is full." They watched Willa's angelic-looking sister float across the floor with her latest smitten dance partner. Now nine-and-ten, her younger sister had grown into a beautiful young woman. Addie moved as if on air, her sunny, ethereal disposition a perfect complement to her fair, delicate looks.

"She will no doubt make a brilliant match," Willa said. "One can only hope it's not that clod she is dancing with right now."

"That is most unkind." Mother admonished her. "The Earl of Spence comes from a noble ancient family and he has six thousand pounds a year."

"But he is rather clumsy, I have to agree," said Cam returning with lemonade and a conspiratorial wink for Willa.

She sipped her lemonade, the lukewarm liquid doing little to cool her in the growing warmth of the assembly hall. Someone had thrown open the terrace doors, but it didn't seem to make much of a difference because the air remained thick and still. Surveying the hall, her mind wandered as she watched the well-dressed couples take their turn about the dance floor, absentmindedly tapping her slipper to the music. Her foot froze when she saw the scoundrel emerge from the crowd.

Framed by strong shoulders, his towering black-clad form moved with supreme self-assurance, like a god who'd descended from Mount Olympus to walk among lesser beings. He strode across the room in a way that was both leisurely and aggressive, exuding an unmistakable air of dominion. She pretended to ignore him, as if that were really possible, and prayed he wouldn't see her. But the beast cut a path straight toward her; his long, strong legs moved with determined purpose, eating up the distance between them.

Her stomach plummeted. There was no escape.

"Preston, you nonesuch, however are you?" Cam said when the beastly man came to a stop before them. "I was beginning to think you meant to stay abroad forever." Cam clapped his hand on the stranger's shoulder and shook his hand with vigor.

Willa's mouth fell open. This Mr. Preston person was clearly known to Cam, who seemed quite pleased to see him. There'd be no avoiding the scoundrel now.

"Ladies, allow me to present His Grace, the Duke of Hartwell."

She jerked back. A duke! It was unimaginable.

"This is my aunt, the Dowager Marchioness of Camryn." Cam turned to Willa. "And my cousin, Lady Wilhelmina Stanhope."

The duke greeted them most properly, except for the

glint in his dark eyes when he bowed over Willa's gloved hand. She curtseyed—perhaps not as deeply as one should for a duke—and murmured the usual polite salutations, all the while taking care to avoid his gaze. But once he returned his attention to Cam, she stole a closer look.

He couldn't exactly be considered handsome—his features were too vivid for that. They were like sharp-cut glass, giving him an almost harsh appearance. He wore his dark mane unfashionably long and tied back at the nape of his neck, which emphasized his bold features.

"For shame, Camryn," Mother was saying. "How is it that you haven't made His Grace known to us before now?"

"Preston has been abroad." He turned to the duke. "Although I suppose you are Hartwell now since you've come into the title. Must I address you as 'Your Grace'?"

"Hardly," the duke said in a dry tone. "Hartwell will do nicely."

"The duke and I were up at Cambridge together," Cam said. "We had some good times, didn't we, Pres…errr… Hartwell?"

"Indeed." The duke's smile softened the severe angles of his face. "However, I fear there is little we can say of it in front of gentle company."

"No doubt," Willa said tartly. The words slipped out almost before she realized she'd spoken aloud. Mother gasped at the insolence.

"Touché, Lady Wilhelmina." Mirth lit the duke's eyes, which had seemed black at first, but were actually a midnight blue. They crinkled up at the corners when he smiled. "It appears you know your cousin quite well."

"Willa is hard on me." Good humor filled Cam's voice.

"I suppose this is how it feels to have a sister."

"And quite a lovely sister at that," Hartwell said. "I see the next set is about to begin. Perhaps I could have the honor of dancing with Lady Wilhelmina?"

Willa drew back. "I am complimented, Your Grace. But I find the dancing has quite worn me out."

"Nonsense." Barely-controlled excitement caused Mother to fidget as though she needed to use the chamber pot. "You were saying you'd like another turn around the dance floor and, fortunately for His Grace, you have room on your dance card."

Willa suppressed a sigh. She'd said no such thing. But standing up with someone of Hartwell's consequence would be quite the achievement for a girl who'd teetered on the brink of ruination for as long as she had.

"There you have it then." The duke favored Mother with a heart-stoppingly wide smile, revealing an orderly row of long bright teeth, except for a couple of renegades which tilted their own way. His twinkling eyes settled expectantly on Willa as if defying her to disappoint her own mother.

Drat it all. "As you wish." Willa forced indifference into her voice.

"Excellent!" Mother clasped her hands together, her face glowing with delighted anticipation. "Do enjoy yourselves."

As fortune would have it, the next dance was another waltz. She shivered when the duke placed a firm hand on her waist, taking her gloved hand in the other as they joined the crowd of dancers on the floor. His solid strength encased her, making her feel strangely safe and protected.

"Alone at last," he said.

"Indeed." Slipping behind the protective mask of

detachment she often donned in public, Willa gazed about the room, adopting a deliberate pose of polite disinterest.

• • •

Grey Preston, Duke of Hartwell, cocked one eyebrow, both amused and disconcerted by Lady Wilhelmina's show of disdain. That didn't happen to him often, especially now that he'd come into the title. Still, her cool distance gave him a chance to examine her more closely.

She was exquisite. Much of her beauty came from the incandescent quality of her skin. Smooth and flawless, the soft, porcelain-like surface seemed to glow from within. His gaze moved from the graceful turn of throat to the smooth expanse of her fashionable décolletage, which revealed the creamy slopes of generous breasts.

His blood warmed. He couldn't blame Bellingham for being besotted with such an extraordinary creature. Contrary to what she'd assumed, he'd heard only snatches of the exchange on the terrace. The word *marriage* had certainly been bandied about several times. His stomach tightened with disgust at the thought of Gus Manning laying a hand on her person. Surely, Cam would never allow such a sordid match. But how could she not be married by now? She must have had numerous offers. Her obvious beauty easily eclipsed all of the other, less fortunate maidens in the room.

She regarded him with impossibly large eyes, which dominated her face, their velvety mocha color alight with intelligence. "It seems I should thank you for not referring to our….ah…earlier encounter outside."

"Do not think of it. It is I who should apologize for discomfiting you." He paused. "Might I ask if Bellingham is a serious suitor?"

"Most assuredly not. I hadn't seen him in years before this evening." She had a voice like melted dark chocolate — creamy, vibrant, and smoothly potent. "Are you acquainted with the earl?"

"We were at Cambridge together."

The lines of her body stiffened. "So you are friends."

"No." He resisted the urge to make a rude sound. "One could not call us friends. Although it appears the same could not be said about the two of you. Bellingham does seem quite enamored of you."

"It is nothing."

"From what I overheard on the terrace, Gus would disagree. It is easy to comprehend why he remains besotted with you. You are uniquely lovely."

Especially given the intriguing strands of red and gold which lit her chestnut curls, dancing each time they fleetingly caught the light. His gaze fell to the enticing plumpness of her moist, pink lips. "Perhaps Byron thought of you when he wrote his latest poem, 'She walks in beauty, like the night. Of cloudless climes and starry nights.'"

The lady blushed. "Are you a poet as well as a world traveler, Your Grace?"

"Not at all." The lovely flush of color against her luminescent complexion entranced him. How charming that someone of such extreme loveliness could remain so modest. "It is your beauty that inspires me to quote poetry."

"I believe Lord Byron wrote that poem for his betrothed wife," she said coolly.

"A beauty such as yours would inspire thoughts of matrimony." Taking such an exquisite creature to wife wouldn't be any hardship. He could easily see her as a duchess. With all of that icy majesty, she already carried herself like a queen.

Her face reddened at his shameless flirtation, the flush on her cheeks extending to the delicate curves of her ears. "Camryn says you've been living abroad." Wintry eyes scanned his face. "Might I ask where?"

He smiled at her obvious attempt to change the subject. "India."

Her breath caught and her liquid eyes warmed with interest in a way that made Hartwell's body tighten in one quick surge. "India!" she exclaimed, all of that haughty distance falling away. "You are so very fortunate. Someday, I plan to travel to the faraway places I've read about. I long to see India and Greece and Italy."

"Surely such a thing is not done by young maidens."

"It won't be long before I am considered so long in the tooth, no one will have a care what I do."

He couldn't imagine that. "Perhaps your husband will show you the world."

"Tell me of India. It seems such an exotic place."

He thought of the bazaars, hot and crowded with masses of people thronging forward, the air thick with heat and dust, redolent with the smell of unwashed bodies, sultry spices, and incense. Perhaps it was the cacophony of sounds he remembered most: the clatter of a cart, the noise of fast-talking shopkeepers bargaining their way to a sale.

"There is nothing plain or bland about the country or its people," he answered. "It is a country of extremes, the hottest of weather, and a rainy season that seems to go on forever. The food can be so spicy it burns all the way down to your stomach. The sweets are almost too sugary to countenance."

To his astonishment, she smiled, her face relaxing into a deliciously warm expression which reminded him of the sun shining down on a spring garden. "How vividly you describe it."

Surrendering to the temptation to bask in her radiance, he leaned closer. She smelled of roses, earthy and rich, yet elusive somehow. Heat flooded his belly. "'I am pale with longing for my beloved.'"

She drew back. "I beg your pardon?"

"It is poetry from India. Centuries old. However, you needn't worry. There's nothing romantic about it. I believe it refers to a love of God."

The chill returned to her voice. "I must say, Your Grace, I find this conversation most forward and unconventional."

"Ah, but then you do not seem conventional, my lady."

She stilled. "If that is intended as another insult—"

"Not at all," he assured her, resisting the impulse to kiss her senseless, to chip away at that icy exterior and revel in that flash of sun he'd glimpsed. "I find most young ladies of the ton to be quite boring and silly. Qualities, I might add, which I would never attribute to you." He was rewarded with another one of those pink blushes which extended to her ears.

"Your Grace, you overstep."

"My apologies then. It would seem, Lady Wilhelmina, that we have gotten off to a most inauspicious start." And then, because he couldn't resist the urge to tease her, "Though I must say it has been most enlightening."

"I sincerely doubt that." Her glistening eyes slid away to resume a wandering look of polite boredom, leaving him feeling strangely bereft.

Chapter Three

"Surely one of the gentlemen from last evening captured your interest," Mother insisted to Addie the following day as they sat in the upstairs drawing room.

Addie reclined lazily on the chaise in front of the window. "All of the gentlemen on my dance card were beyond boring."

"The Earl of Spence seemed taken with you," Mother pressed. "And he has six thousand pounds a year."

"I don't care about that." Turning to where Willa sat by the fire with the *Times of London*, Addie asked, "What are you reading that is of such interest?"

Willa looked up, happy to help her sister distract their marriage-minded mother from her favorite topic. "The *Times* is going on about the waltz again, referring to it as an obscenity."

"Did someone say obscenity?" Cam strode into the room. "I seem to miss all of the most fascinating conversations."

"The *Times* is denouncing the waltz again."

Cam accepted lemonade from Mother and settled opposite the fireplace in the large comfortable chair he favored. Smythe, the butler, appeared in the doorway with a massive bouquet of roses in every shade imaginable; soft pinks, elegant ivory, and vibrant reds with thick, velvety petals which infused the air with their rich scent.

"Wilhelmina, they are for you," Mother said as she read the card, excitement tingeing her words. "It seems you have an admirer."

Her heart stumbled. She hadn't told anyone about seeing Augustus last night. Now it seemed the flowers would do it for her. She pushed to her feet and forced herself to reach for the card her mother held out.

"Oh." She expelled the breath she'd been holding. "They are from Hartwell." With the impudent duke at least, there was nothing to explain, no uncomfortable past to exhume.

Cam cocked an eyebrow. "Hartwell sent you flowers?"

"Perhaps he means to court her." Her mother fidgeted on the sofa. "Wilhelmina is a lady of fine family as well as great beauty. Why wouldn't a duke want to further an acquaintance with her?"

"Willa, Duchess of Hartwell." Mischief danced in Addie's eyes. "It does have a certain ring to it."

"Don't be ridiculous," she said. "I am no great beauty and a duke would never show any real interest in me." Even if Mother chose to ignore the truth, everyone knew that dukes desired brides with impeccable reputations.

Mother turned to Cam. "Tell us about His Grace. You appear to know him well."

"He's the best of men. Fair, honorable, and decent. He

abhors any manner of injustice."

"You make him sound like a paragon." Willa thought of the cad's scurrilous behavior on the terrace. "Surely, he cannot be so perfect."

"All men possess faults. Hartwell does have a temper on him." He drank from his lemonade. "At least he did at Cambridge. I haven't seen him in years. He's been in India."

Mother frowned. "Whatever for?"

"Some business concern." Cam regarded her over the rim of his glass. "Hart is the second son. He never expected to inherit, but his brother the duke died unexpectedly without issue last year."

"Oh, that's dreadful." Mother's sympathetic words were at odds with the undercurrent of excitement in her voice.

Smythe reappeared. "My lord, you have a caller."

Cam smiled and winked at Willa. "Speak of the devil… the duke then?"

The butler's face registered just a touch of confusion before resuming its usual expressionless mask. "Pardon, my lord, but 'tis the Earl of Bellingham who has come to call."

"The Earl of Bellingham?" Startled, Cam flashed a quick look around the parlor.

Augustus. Willa's mouth went dry.

"The old earl?" Mother's gaze darted between Willa and Cam. "What could he mean by coming here?"

"The old earl is dead," Cam told her. "I received word of it last evening. It is his eldest son, Augustus Manning, the new earl, who awaits my pleasure."

Mother's eyes widened. "Perhaps he means to set matters to rights now that his father has passed." Addie straightened on the chaise, her eyes alert with interest, her cheeks tinged with color.

"Very well, Smythe." Cam stood, straightening his cravat as he strode toward the door. "Please show his lordship into my study. I shall receive him there." Relief flooded Willa. Cam meant to spare her any discomfort by conducting the meeting in private.

"Willa," her mother said after Cam left, "why do you suppose he has come to call so soon after the old earl's death?"

Her pulse galloped. "I haven't any idea." Addie coughed and her eyes shifted from her mother to Willa.

"Very well, then." Mother forced a cheery note into her voice. "In due time, Camryn will inform us of the reason for the earl's visit. Until then, we shall not let it concern us." She picked up her needlepoint and appeared to concentrate on her stitching. Following her mother's lead, Willa returned to her newspaper, trying to ignore the painful pounding of her heart and the distraction of Addie pacing about the salon.

Her mind filled with memories of the inn, when the unthinkable had transformed their innocent attachment into something unsavory and shameful. She should tell Mother about her encounter with Augustus last night. The rational part of her mind comprehended marriage to an earl would restore her good name. Mother would no doubt pressure her to accept in order to bury the rumors for good, but her stomach twisted with disgust at the thought of it.

"It would seem" —Cam said when he returned some thirty minutes later— "that a marriage is to take place."

Anxiety arrowed up her spine. She steeled herself, taking a deep breath before bringing her eyes up to meet Cam's. To her surprise, his steady gaze was fixed on Addie.

"Bellingham came to call on behalf of his younger brother, Horace. It seems young Horace is smitten with Addie and feels quite certain the lady in question returns his affections."

Willa whipped around to look at her sister. "You and Race?"

Cam frowned. "Who is Race?"

Mother rose from the sofa, her eyes fixed on Addie. "Horace, the second son," she said. "He is called Race by some."

Addie turned to them from where she stood at the window. She'd gone pale. Chewing her lower lip, a stricken expression crossed her face.

"Well….it's…I supposed," Addie stammered, looking down at her hands.

"What is it you wish to say?" Cam's tone was gentle and reassuring. "Please speak frankly."

Addie took a deep breath. "I am in love with Race Manning and I have been since I was twelve." The words rushed out as though she wanted to declare herself before losing her nerve. "We renewed our acquaintance at the ball last evening. It is my wish to wed him." She walked to where Willa sat on the sofa and dropped down to the floor before her, placing her hands over older sister's. "But I will not accept him if it will hurt or embarrass you after what… his brother did to you." Addie flushed at the awkward reference to Willa's damaged reputation. "I would die before subjecting you to that again. A word from you and I shall send him away."

Addie and Race? In love? Focusing on her sister's face, her heart twinged at the distress she saw there. She glanced up to find Mother and Cam watching with concern etched in their expressions. She shook herself out of her stupor and confusion. "Darling, Addie." She stroked her sister's hair. "Do you truly love him?"

"I do." Willa saw tears in Addie's eyes and felt them sting her own. It all began to make sense to her. She thought back to their summers and realized with a start that Addie and Race had always been together. Sitting near each other, sharing an apple or a private laugh. Willa remembered Race as a brash, but likeable and earnest young man and could well envision him as a kind and loving husband to her sister.

She took a deep breath. "Addie, if you love Race Manning and wish to wed him, then of course you should. All I desire is your happiness." She tugged Addie up off the floor to sit next to her on the sofa. "If Race can provide you with that, I shall be truly happy for you."

"I don't know." Mother looked to Cam. "It is decidedly uncomfortable, considering the past."

"An alliance between the families could serve to put the ugly rumors to rest." He crossed his arms over his chest as he thought it out. "It would surely make people realize the talk surrounding Willa and Bellingham is nonsense. We would never countenance joining our families if there was any truth to it."

Willa pressed her lips together. "It is true enough, Cam."

Surprise lit his face at her directness. A savage expression replaced it. "It is not too late to call him out. Had I been aware of it back then, I most certainly would have."

But Cam had not even been here. He'd been at his own family home several hours away and hadn't heard the rumors until much later, well after her father died and he'd come into the title. When it had been far too late to salvage her reputation.

"Nonsense. That would have created a scandal from which none of us would have recovered." Mother's voice firmed. "Cam has the right of it. A betrothal between our families will put the rumors to rest. We'll put this unfortunate business behind us once and for all."

Once Mother got an idea into her head, it was impossible to dislodge. Willa put an arm around her sister's shoulders. "I suppose felicitations are in order."

Cam turned his attention to Addie. "When, pray tell, did all of this come to pass?"

"He was there last night." Adela's eyes shone. "For the longest time, we presumed there was no hope for our union since—" Her words stumbled and she glanced at her sister.

"Continue," Willa urged, ignoring the tightness in her chest, which always accompanied any reference to her ruination. "The past is the past. What occurred between Augustus and me has no bearing whatsoever on you and Race."

Addie took a breath. "We had always promised each other we would be together. I had not allowed myself to hope that he felt the same way after all these years, but he does."

Smythe reappeared. "Another caller, my lord. It is His Grace, the Duke of Hartwell."

"Ah, this time it is Hart." Tension left Cam's face and he flashed an amused look in Willa's direction. "Please show him in, Smythe."

She sighed, resigning herself to the fact that this was going to be one of those days.

Her smile widening, Mother patted her hair into place. "A duke no less," she said, her voice triumphant. "An excellent match."

An impish look lit Addie's face. "Perhaps it will be a double wedding: Race and I, Willa and her duke." She jumped to her feet and dropped into a deep curtsey before Willa. "Your Grace."

She fired a withering glare at Addie. "Stop it, both of you. There is no hope of a match. He is probably here to see Cam."

Cam gave her a wicked smile. "I suppose that is possible. But then again, the flowers were not for me. Ah, Hartwell," he said, rising from his seat to greet Grey Preston. "How nice of you to call."

Hartwell strode in, his tall dark presence immediately asserting itself in the room. Willa wondered if he always looked so immaculate. Except for his artfully tied white cravat, the duke had cloaked his masculine frame in unrelenting black again. His midnight hair was tied back in a perfect queue, the shine on his Hessians so bright she could see her reflection in them.

He presented a bouquet of spring flowers to Mother, which she accepted with great flourish. "Why thank you, Your Grace! They are lovely." She turned to Smythe. "Please find a vase for this. And see about refreshment for the duke." Turning back to Hartwell, she gestured with her hand. "Please, Your Grace, do have a seat. You honor us with your visit."

After greeting everyone, the duke settled into a chair. Looking beyond Willa, he spied the generous bouquet of flowers. "Excellent. I see you received my flowers."

"Yes, indeed! They are beautiful, Your Grace," Mother gushed, before turning a pointed eye toward her daughter. "Aren't they, Wilhelmina?"

"Yes. You really shouldn't have."

"Nonsense. It is my great pleasure." Amusement laced the polite tones of his full-bodied voice. "Although, of course, the loveliest bloom pales next to Lady Wilhelmina's radiance."

"Oh, my." Mother put a hand to her chest. "You are too kind."

"Yes." Willa hoped her mother wouldn't swoon to the floor right there at the pointed toes of the Duke's gleaming black boots. "Far too kind."

"Not at all." A roguish glint lit his eyes. "Few diamonds sparkle as brightly as you, my lady."

"Your Grace flatters me greatly." She winced inwardly, certain her burning ears were the same shade as the crimson roses behind her. She had no idea how to respond to the duke's flirtatious flattery. Having spent little time in society and even less with courtly gentlemen, the rules of coquettish behavior escaped her.

Fortunately, Smythe's appearance with the refreshments rescued her for the moment. Eyeing the artful arrangement of delicate sandwiches, meat pies, cheeses, biscuits, small cakes, and pastries, she noted the kitchen staff had gone out of its way to impress their prestigious guest on such short notice.

Turning to Hartwell, Mother said, "Tea, Your Grace? Or lemonade?"

"Lemonade, if you please. I am quite partial to it." He flashed that scoundrel's smile in Willa's direction. "I find myself drawn to the paradox of how something so tantalizingly sweet can also be so tart."

The footman entered with the elements necessary for tea. Willa scooted forward to unlock the tea caddy, wondering how anyone could prefer lemonade over tea. Nothing competed with a perfect blend.

The duke's dark brow furrowed. "Lady Wilhelmina brews the tea?"

"No one prepares it like Willa," said Mother. "Although the mistress of the house usually has the honor, I concede to my daughter's obvious mastery."

Feeling Hartwell's eyes upon her, Willa opened the caddy and selected from among the special variety of leaves. Once the rich distinctive aroma of fermented tea leaves wafted into the air, she promptly forgot all about the duke and everything else. Her senses alert and engaged, she concentrated on her preparation, the calming sensation of formulating the perfect brew settling deep in her bones. She measured an ideal mix of green and black leaves from China before adding her own distinctive ingredients—a bit of dried orange rind, a hint of rosemary, and pinch of cinnamon. She frowned to see they'd brought out the silver teapot. China teapots produced better-tasting brews, but allowances had to be made when a duke came to call.

She added the mixed tea leaves to the pre-warmed pot and nodded for the footman to pour boiling water over them. The humid steam drifted upward, carrying the beginnings of the brew's aromatic scent. Willa inhaled, both savoring and assessing the aroma. She closed the top of the teapot and wrapped a cloth around it to seal in the heat during the brewing process.

Satisfied the tea was steeping properly, she looked up to find Hartwell's inky blue eyes studying her as if he could see right into her soul. Her skin tingled and her heart thudded. Mesmerized, she couldn't look away.

"Willa." Mother's voice seemed to come from very far away. "Have I told you Lady Barnes is desperate for your tea recipe with thyme in it?"

Hartwell blinked, breaking eye contact, and Willa started breathing again.

The duke cleared his throat. "Perhaps I will take tea after all."

"Excellent choice," Cam said. "Once you've tasted Willa's tea, none other will satisfy you."

"No doubt," murmured Hartwell.

Willa's ears burned. "One lump or two, Your Grace?"

"Three, if you please." His piercing gaze held hers. "I have a tendency toward overindulgence."

Suddenly remembering the tea, she gaped blindly at the pot, unable to recall how long she'd let it brew. She poured the steaming dark amber liquid into each cup, hoping she'd timed it properly. At least the brandied color appeared correct. The pungent smell of fresh tea, with a hint of citrus coupled with the sharpness of rosemary, filled the air, satisfying the senses. She counted out three lumps for the duke and then moved onto her family members, taking care to prepare each cup according to their individual tastes. She watched out of the corner of her eye as Hartwell took his first sip.

He sniffed it, very subtly, but Willa caught the almost undetectable action because she always did the same herself. Then he tasted it.

"Excellent," he pronounced. "Full bodied and aromatic with a slightly tangy finish."

Warmth spread through her, and it had nothing to do with the tea since she hadn't sampled hers yet. Taking a sip, she could only agree with his assessment. Her special concoction tasted full and lively on the tongue, with just the right touch of astringency.

Cam reached for a sandwich. "Hartwell, I was telling the ladies that you were in India."

Mother crossed both hands flat over her chest. "Yes, how exotic, Your Grace." Willa fought to keep from rolling her eyes at the way her mother fawned all over the duke. No doubt he was accustomed to toadyish behavior from females, especially marriage-minded mommas like hers.

Cam leaned forward. "What business did you have there?"

"I traded mostly in sugar."

"Will you continue that endeavor, now that you have returned permanently to England?" Cam asked.

"Indeed. My man of business is seeing about purchasing an adequate building to house my clerks and business concerns here in Town."

"How did your trade affect the locals?" Willa knew from her reading that many Englishmen made their fortune in India at the expense of native workers. "Was it successful for them as well?"

"Willa!" Mother gasped, shooting her a daggered look. "Your Grace, my daughter means no offense to be sure."

"Not to worry. I'm certain I comprehend your daughter's true intentions perfectly," he said easily. "To demonstrate that I hold no ill feelings, perhaps Lady Wilhelmina would favor me with a carriage ride through Hyde Park." His smooth smile almost dared her to refuse. "If she is disposed, of course."

Willa stiffened. She would decline all right. She wanted nothing further to do with men—especially one who seemed to enjoy mocking her. "That is most kind of you, Your Grace. But truly, we have had much family excitement here today and I am disposed to take an afternoon nap." Mother would think her still emotional over Addie's news and playing on her softhearted nature would give Willa a chance to bow out of an afternoon ride with Hartwell.

"Actually, I was hoping you could join me on the morrow, provided the marchioness approves."

"Of course!" Her mother jumped in before Willa could respond. "I would be most pleased. We both would."

"Willa adores riding in the park," Addie piped in, wide-eyed.

Willa suppressed the urge to massage her temples. She lacked the energy to continue playing whatever game the duke had in mind. At least if she agreed to accompany him, he might depart posthaste. And an afternoon ride with His Grace promised to be passably more tolerable than another encounter with Augustus. Race would no doubt call upon his betrothed soon. And his brother might well accompany him.

"Why ever not." She feigned indifference. "Unless Camryn has an objection?" She cast a hopeful look in her cousin's direction.

Cam grinned. "Not at all, dearest cousin."

"Excellent," said Hartwell. "I shall look forward to it."

Chapter Four

"May I be frank?" Willa said the following day as she and the duke rode in his impressive phaeton, a high-perched, black lacquer conveyance.

"Do you have any other manner of speaking?" Hartwell kept his eyes on the road ahead. "Or do you save that particular privilege solely for me?"

"In all seriousness, why are you doing this?"

"Taking you for a carriage ride?"

"Seeking me out to amuse yourself."

"Perhaps I mean to court you." He fired off a slow confident smile that made her heart skid. Bold and forceful, it was devastating in its allure. There was something almost animalistic in those decisive rows of long teeth.

She forced herself to remember a duke would never court someone with her past—especially one as appealing as the man sitting next to her. Unless, of course, he'd yet to hear of the scandal. "Why, pray tell, would you engage with someone such as me?"

"Someone such as you?" His dark brows furrowed. "Granted, one risks frostbite from that icy tongue of yours, but I daresay I can withstand the cold."

"And you do have all of that hot air to keep you warm," she said sweetly.

He barked a laugh. "That, along with the certain knowledge that summer invariably follows winter. I look forward with great anticipation to the hot and sultry season."

"I am obviously on the shelf," she said firmly. "Meanwhile, there are ambitious mothers all over Town who would be thrilled to have the Duke of Hartwell court their daughters."

"Your mother seems pleased enough."

"She tends to be swayed by a grand title, with little regard as to the character of the man who carries it."

"Brrrr." He gave an exaggerated shiver. "I do believe a frosty gale has just blown over me."

Suppressing a smile, she inhaled, drawing his masculine scent into her lungs. He must have restrained from cheroots thus far today. He had that clean, strong—very pleasing—smell again. "As you can see, I am neither an impressionable young debutante nor a desperate ape leader to be toyed with." Nor a strumpet who dallied with dukes because of a dented reputation. "So it seems you are wasting your time."

"On the contrary, I enjoy myself immensely in your company." His midnight blue gaze perused her with open appreciation. "I'm even coming to appreciate the nippy air."

Perspiration beaded on her upper lip. Botheration, the man's flirtations made her nervous and her insides seemed to be vibrating. "Is that why you mock me?"

"Mock you? Not at all, though I must admit I enjoy

sparring with you."

"If it is a sparring partner you seek, perhaps you should repair to the nearest boxing club," she retorted.

Hartwell laughed out loud, a full-bodied sound which rumbled from deep within his chest. He threw his head back, his profile emphasizing a strong nose and sharp-cut cheeks. Drawn to the sound of his laugh, she couldn't resist a slight smile.

"I assure you boxing is the furthest activity from my mind when I am with you," he drawled.

Willa's cheeks and ears burned. He had an annoying knack of doing that to her. "Honestly, Your Grace."

"Please, you must call me Hartwell." He cast her a sidelong glance. "Surely, we are well acquainted enough to dispense with this 'Your Grace' business."

"That would be improper as you well know." She tried to ignore the way her heart danced around inside her chest. "I can endure your antics, but you are shamelessly toying with my mother."

He sobered. "I beg your pardon?"

"Surely you have noticed she is quite taken with the notion that a duke might be interested in courting me at my advanced age. It is cruel of you to give her false hope."

Hartwell drew back. "I would never be deliberately cruel to a lady such as your mother. Why do you presume there is anything false in my pursuit?" Pulling the phaeton to a stop in the park, he turned to give Willa his full attention.

The sincere interest shining in those dark blue depths prompted a glowing sensation in her chest, but she forced herself to remember Hartwell would soon learn the *ton* considered her to be damaged goods. The cool mask slipped back into place. "It appears, Your Grace, that your stay in India has left you quite behind the times."

• • •

That evening, with his thoughts still full of the ice queen, Hartwell ventured out to Brooks, the London gentlemen's club on St. James Street. So much about Wilhelmina Stanhope perplexed him.

Your stay in India has left you quite behind the times. He'd seen Willa retreat back behind that impenetrable façade. What had she meant? Why did she assume his intentions were less than honorable? Clearly, she didn't comprehend the depth of her physical appeal. Just a glance from those endless velvet eyes would bring any red-blooded man to a point. He had a mind to warm her right up, kindling a fire in those immense eyes. Anything to burn away the controlled, shuttered look she hid behind.

Your stay in India has left you quite behind the times.

A lady of her undeniable beauty shouldn't still be unmarried at her age. Unless, of course, she'd waited for Bellingham. The thought of it roiled his gut.

Arriving at Brooks, he strode across the club's plush carpets into the gaming room where a fire roared in the immense marble hearth. The low murmur of voices, punctuated by occasional bursts of muted laughter, wafted through the smoke-hazed room, the air redolent with the smell of burning tobacco and men's shaving soap.

"Hartwell, you old nabob, I see you've found your way back from India," said David Selwyn, an old friend from Cambridge. "Have you finally tired of building your empire?"

"Not at all." He wasn't one to stay idle for long. As a second son, necessity had driven him to make his fortune in India. Now, as duke, desire fueled his continued interest in enterprise. Few things got his blood pumping more than negotiating a lucrative transaction. "However, my ducal responsibilities require that I move the headquarters of said empire to London." Hartwell joined the table, settling into a plush brown leather chair, and nodding a greeting to the others at the table, all of whom he had some acquaintance with from their university days.

"I say, was that you escorting Lady Wilhelmina Stanhope in the park today?" garbled Lord Edmund Garrick, whose tongue was known to get a little loose when he drank too much.

"It was. Although I don't see why that would be of any interest to you." He spoke in a curt tone, unwilling to discuss a lady in these surroundings.

"Brave of you," Garrick mumbled under his breath.

He lifted his chin. "Why is that?"

Sir Heenan, a thin gentleman with premature gray at his temples, leaned forward. "You've been away, Hartwell."

"Meaning?"

"Meaning there is a quiet understanding among gentlemen of a certain standing that Lady Wilhelmina is spoken for."

"By whom?" To his surprise, Hart's gut twisted. "I was not aware the lady is betrothed."

"They say Bellingham has put his mark on her." Garrick's words tumbled out in one continuous slur.

Hart's fingers tightened around his glass. "What the

devil are you implying?"

"Shut up, Garrick," Selwyn said tightly. "You really can be an arse sometimes."

"There's long been talk of her belonging to Augustus Manning. He's finally come into the title. He's Bellingham now," Heenan said. "Surely you remember him from Cambridge."

"Vaguely."

Remembrance clicked in Heenan's eyes. "Ah, yes, there was bad blood between the two of you."

"I'll say." Garrick bottomed out his glass. "Hartwell gave Bellingham the thrashing of his life. They'd have sent him up if he hadn't been the son of a duke."

"You never did say what Bellingham did to deserve such harsh treatment," Heenan said.

Hart concentrated on the swirling brandy in his glass. "No, I did not."

Heenan added, "Brave of you to lick the heir to an earldom."

Garrick motioned for more brandy. A club worker stepped forward with a full decanter. "Especially considering you were only a second son with no hope of a title." He raised his refilled drink in salute. "Congratulations, by the way, on your reversal of fortune."

Hart's chest constricted at the indirect reference to his late brother. Michael's kind and steady visage flashed in his mind. A good man's untimely death was no cause for celebration. Looking to Heenan, he said, "I scarcely see how Lady Wilhelmina can belong to Bellingham if there is no betrothal."

"There is certain talk no gentleman would ever repeat."

Heenan reached for his mother-of-pearl snuffbox. "Some say it is why the lady has kept herself away from Town for so long."

"And this is commonly discussed in society?"

"It is not the kind of thing one hears in Mayfair's drawing rooms," Selwyn answered in halting tones.

"But most gentlemen about Town eventually hear the talk," Garrick added with a lascivious smirk.

Heenan leaned over and inhaled snuff into his nose. "Not that anyone dares to cut her in public." Leaning back in his chair with a satisfied sigh, he used a handkerchief to wipe remnants of the powdery substance from his upper lip. "Impeccable family lines and all. The family carries on as though nothing has happened. She is under the protection of her cousin, the Marquess of Camryn, who is quite influential in the Lords. No one dares risk his wrath."

"I don't follow."

Garrick leaned forward. "They say the chit is compromised. Utterly and completely, if you get my meaning." He winked at Hart. "But she still acts the frigid princess, all high and mighty. Otherwise, who wouldn't want to toss up those skirts and give her a good hard—"

Something in his head snapped loose, blinding him to anything but the desire to crush the drunken whoreson beneath his boot heel. He bolted to his feet and shoved the table back with a loud clatter. Towering over Garrick, he grabbed the man's cravat with one hand and drew back his fist with the other. Garrick shrank back in his chair, wide-eyed, his face pinched with fear. Action at the other gaming tables screeched to a halt. Silence descended; all eyes were riveted on Hartwell.

Selwyn jumped up and placed a calming hand on his shoulder. "Now Hartwell," he said, partially positioning himself between the two men. "This is just a friendly misunderstanding among gentlemen."

His neck burned. It was a lie. It had to be. "It is hardly the act of a gentleman to insult a lady's honor in the most grievous way possible."

"My sincere apologies, H-Hartwell. I d-did not know the l-lady was of a-any import to you," Garrick stuttered, still cowering in his seat.

"It seems I've arrived just in time for the real games to begin."

The familiar jocular voice pierced the red fog enveloping Hartwell. He glanced over his shoulder to see Cam approaching their table.

"What is this?" The marquess handed his greatcoat to one of the club workers. "Causing trouble already, Hartwell?"

His head screamed with anger, consuming him with an overwhelming desire to break the lying bastard's short neck with his bare hands. But he struggled to get a hold of his temper. Cam had appeared. Too many eyes were upon him. To allow this scene to play out would no doubt spark gossip about what had been said. He felt strangely protective and unwilling to subject Willa's reputation to such potential ruin.

"Camryn, jolly good to see you," said Selwyn, appearing hopeful that Cam's appearance would put an end to the confrontation.

Hart reluctantly released Garrick with a small shove. Lowering his fist, he dragged his eyes from Garrick's ashen face and turned to Cam, struggling to mask his fury. "No trouble. Just a misunderstanding among gentlemen." He forced a cool tone despite the fire raging inside him. "Garrick here was just about to leave us. Won't you take his seat?"

The little bastard sprang to his feet, eager to take his cue. "Absolutely. I must make haste and depart. Your servant, Camryn," he uttered, gathering his things before scrambling out of the room.

Cam shook his head as he watched Garrick leave. "Lord, I see you still know how to clear a room, Hartwell." He settled in to the departed man's seat. "I haven't seen Garrick move that quickly since Eton and perhaps not even then."

"He's a fool. Hardly worth my time." A slow burn still oozed through his veins. "Enough talk." He reached for the deck of cards. "Let's get back to the real action, shall we?"

• • •

"I do believe this is the best tea I have ever tasted," Octavia Gordon declared as she put her teacup down.

"Would you care for more?" Willa smiled when Octavia held out her teacup. Her first attempt at hosting a meeting of the Ladies' Reading Society had turned out to be a success so far. She enjoyed the women in this group. Their thoughts might be shocking to some but Willa relished the discussions.

"Willa is the tea goddess." Flor held out her cup for more as well. "People actually try to buy her special blends, but it would never do for a young lady to be involved in trade," she said with mock horror.

"The judgment of society is meant to keep women from reaching their full potential," said Pamela Grenfell, a pale sliver of a woman with a hand at her graceful, long white neck. "It's just as Mary Wollstonecraft says."

"Her thoughts are quite astounding in their directness," Willa said.

"But true, nonetheless," said Pamela. "Take your situation as an example. Just because you were seen at an inn in the company of the future Earl of Bellingham, your reputation is damaged."

Willa sipped her tea to hide her discomfort. Yet the frankness of these discussions was what drew her to these women.

"And there is no stain on Bellingham," said Octavia. "Now there's a cad, if there ever was one. It's completely unjust."

"The Duke of Hartwell does not seem to mind her reputation," Flor said with a naughty grin.

"Do tell." Eyes wide, Pamela tilted her head toward Willa. "Is Hartwell courting you?"

"Of course not." Her cheeks heated. "His Grace called once, but that is because he and Camryn are the oldest of friends."

"They danced a waltz at Almack's," Flor said dreamily. "He is very appealing."

"His Grace?" Octavia frowned. "He is a frightening sort if you ask me."

Willa resisted an immediate urge to defend the duke. "Why do you say so?"

"Everyone knows he has an uncontrollable temper," said Octavia. "He thrashed Bellingham almost to the death when they were at university."

Pamela nodded. "My brother Freddie was a year behind them. He says Hartwell almost got sent up for it."

"Why would he do such a thing?" Willa asked.

"According to my Freddie, Hartwell would never say what triggered the beating." Pamela placed her cup in its saucer with a delicate clink. "Bellingham has always maintained Hartwell was jealous because he was only a second son while Bellingham stood to inherit an earldom."

Flor shook her head. "I can't imagine that man being jealous of anyone. He carries himself as though he owns the town."

"According to Freddie, Hartwell was superior to Bellingham in every other way—in their studies and physical pursuits," Pamela said.

"At least that part of the story is easily believed." Willa could not imagine Hartwell assaulting someone out of jealousy. If true, it did not speak well of his character.

Pamela held out her cup. "More tea, if you please. It is excellent." Willa obliged somewhat absentmindedly— her thoughts busy with the animus between Hartwell and Augustus.

"This is heavenly," Pamela said between sips of tea. "You truly could sell it. Willa's talent at blending tea could be a way for her to support herself without depending upon a man. So why should she not be able to do it?"

Octavia leaned forward to put her empty tea cup on the table. "I'll tell you why. Because society prefers to keep women helpless and under the control of men."

Willa had never thought to sell her blends. "Oh, I just mix tea for the pure pleasure of it."

"You could call it Heavenly Tea," Flor said thoughtfully. "It would see a fine profit, to be sure."

Willa smiled, a little uncomfortable with the thought of trade. "Camryn has put aside a most generous portion even if I never marry. I've no need of income if I live modestly."

"But there are those who do." Octavia gave Flor a meaningful look. "Are you thinking what I am thinking?"

Excitement shone in Flor's eyes. "That's an excellent idea. It could work."

Willa glanced between the two women. "What could work?"

"You see," said Flor, leaning in toward Willa, "there is a little coffee house that we sponsor."

Willa glanced around at the expectant faces focused on her. "I'm afraid I don't understand."

"It's sort of our little secret," said Pamela. "Our families would not approve."

Willa's eyes rounded in shock. "Are you in trade?" she asked incredulously. Like her, these women had no need of funds. Not only was Flor's father an earl, but Octavia's was a viscount, while the death of Pamela's husband had left her comfortably settled.

"Not exactly." Flor patted her hand. "We help support the coffee shop to give work to women of the lower orders."

"Wives whose husbands have died, or fallen women with children," added Pamela.

"They work at the coffee house so they can earn an honest living without having to sell themselves," said Octavia. "All women should be able to work to help keep their families."

"Octavia rented out the shop and supplied it to begin with, but it isn't making sufficient money to support itself," Flor explained. "And the cost of both tea and sugar is rather high, which makes matters even more difficult."

Octavia nodded. "I cannot continue to support it

indefinitely. It must turn enough of a profit to pay the rent, wages, and supplies. And if we are made to relocate the shop, that would drive up costs considerably."

"Why would you move the coffee house?" Willa asked.

"The landlord, Mr. Webb, has raised the rent twice. Now he informs us that someone intends to purchase the building," Octavia said. "And that the buyer will wish to make use of the entire building for his own business concerns."

"That's where your tea comes in." Excitement infused Flor's words. "It would help considerably with expenses if we sell your special blends, both to partake of at the shop and to carry home. No one would ever have to know where it came from."

Willa couldn't help feeling flattered. The idea of sharing her blends with a wider circle of people held great appeal. Although the excitement in the room was contagious, she struggled to hold on to reason. "But what if we are discovered? It would be the scandal of the season."

"We shall just see to it that we are never discovered," said Flor, her voice resolute.

Willa pondered the possibility. "I could use my pin money for supplies so no one need know."

Flor's face lit up. "Then you will do it?"

"It is a worthwhile cause."

Octavia clapped her hands together. "Excellent!"

The more she thought about it, the more she warmed to the idea. Her expertise with teas could be more than a hobby; it offered a way to do something of real purpose. Excitement bubbled up in her. "I will do it," she said her tone growing more decisive, a sense of freedom billowing up inside of her. Here at last was one aspect of her life that she could take control of. "Where do we start?"

The talk turned to how much tea would be needed and how it would be packaged. They decided Pamela would arrange for a discreet member of her household staff to deliver the tea to the shop. As the hour grew late and her guests prepared to take their leave, it occurred to Willa that the reading group had not discussed a single book during their meeting.

She cast an appraising eye over her new friends. "This is a most unusual Ladies Reading Society."

Pamela brushed a farewell kiss over Willa's cheek. "And we are most happy to have you join us."

Closing the door behind them, she turned around to find Addie coming down the hallway polishing an apple on her sleeve. "Why are you smiling?"

Willa straightened up. "Is it a crime to smile?"

Addie's eyes narrowed. "If I did not know better, I would say you are up to something."

"Me?" She reached for the apple and took a bite. "Do not be ridiculous. You are the adventurous sister." She handed back the apple. "The most exciting thing I've done all week is host the Ladies Reading Society."

Addie rolled her eyes. "True enough. Between all that reading and your tea blending, you really can be quite the bore."

Feeling almost giddy, Willa suppressed the urge to giggle. "Quite right."

Addie bit into her apple and chewed slowly. "So why you do look like the cat who ate the cream?"

"I cannot say." She sailed past her sister with a secret smile. "Read into that what you will."

. . .

Willa smoothed out her pale pink dress as her maid put the finishing touches on her hair. Her unruly chestnut curls were in an upswept style, with some tendrils left loose to frame her face, softening her features, although there was nothing to be done about her overly large mouth and eyes. She certainly would never have her sister's delicate looks.

Still, she'd taken extra care with her appearance this evening and tried to convince herself that it had nothing to do with the Duke of Hartwell being on the guest list. A tap on the door sounded, followed by a beaming Addie.

"Are you quite ready? Mother is asking for us in the drawing room." Addie actually glowed with happiness now that she'd found Race again. She looked as though she could float away at a moment's notice. "You really do look so lovely," Addie said.

"Pish, posh." Willa turned to kiss her sister on the cheek. "It is you who are beautiful."

They were interrupted by a tap at the door. A footman appeared when Willa bid that he enter. "My lady, Mr. Smythe says there is a package you would like sent out?"

She swallowed hard. What unfortunate timing for him to appear at the same time as Addie. Hoping her sister would not suspect anything, she said in an off-hand manner, "Yes, thank you." She pointed to the sizable package containing the tea blends she'd prepared for the first delivery to Pamela. "Please take it to Lady Grenfell."

Addie eyed the package with interest. "What is in it?" she asked after the footman departed.

A guilty ache stirred in Willa's stomach. Although lying did not come easily to her, she forced herself to answer in the same easy manner as before. "Just some books we are exchanging."

"I should have known." Addie groaned. "You are such a bluestocking."

She gave an inward sigh of relief. "Shall we go down then?"

Addie paused, her demeanor turning more serious. "Willa, are you certain this is all right for you?"

"Of course. I am beyond thrilled for you and Race. I see the way he makes you feel."

"Still, because of my betrothal you have to receive his swine of a brother. Has Bellingham called again?"

She resisted the urge to shake out the growing tightness in her shoulders. Augustus had tried to see her twice since arranging Addie and Race's betrothal. The first time, she'd had the good fortune to be out with Flor. When he called again, she instructed Smythe to tell him she was not at home to callers. "If you are referring to Augustus, yes, he has called, but I have not received him. Nor do I intend to in the future."

Addie bit her lip in a familiar nervous gesture. "I've placed you in a terrible spot."

"Nonsense. I am no longer a young silly girl. I have no interest or remaining feelings for Bellingham." Hearing the words spoken aloud made her realize how much she truly meant them. Carrying the weight of the scandal all these years had exhausted her. She finally felt ready—eager even—to put it behind her.

"I cannot abide the man." Addie wrinkled her nose. "He

is far too well pleased with himself. I should think his neck would hurt from constantly sticking his nose in the air."

Willa suppressed a genuine laugh. "Addie, you mustn't say things like that. We are liable to giggle all through dinner."

Addie's left brow rose up into a devilish arch. "Just imagine what the ton will say about those ill-raised Stanhope girls."

Willa slipped her arm through Addie's to guide her toward the door. "Now, let us go enjoy ourselves. This is your betrothal celebration. You must not concern yourself with my feelings a moment longer."

Addie smiled, seeming convinced for the moment that Willa meant what she said. "Well, then, by all means, let us join our guests. They must have arrived by now."

Trying to calm the uneasy feeling that lingered in the pit of her stomach, Willa followed her sister out the door. It dawned on her that the nerves had nothing at all to do with Augustus Manning and everything to do with the perplexing and strangely compelling Duke of Hartwell.

Chapter Five

Hart noticed the moment Willa and her sister entered the room. The man he assumed to be Horace Manning did as well. Bellingham's younger brother lit up at the sight of his betrothed, immediately leaving his brother's side to go to her and offer his arm. They seemed an unlikely couple. The girl's petite, refined looks stood in sharp contrast to her betrothed's thick muscled body and rough-hewn features.

He barely noticed the golden-haired sister even though her fragile features and delicate frame were the *ton*'s ideal of female loveliness. She paled in comparison to the full lushness of Willa's earthy appeal—a mere nymph in the shadow of a robust goddess.

Hart's gaze flitted back to Bellingham, who stood by the fireplace chatting with Cam, one elbow propped on the mantle, a glass of sherry in his hand. It had been years since he'd laid eyes on the man. Gus took a long drink and his silvery eyes locked on Willa as she glided across the room to join a group of ladies on the sofa.

She carried herself magnificently, shoulders drawn back, chin lifted, spine erect. Her blush pink gown enhanced the pale rosiness of her perfect complexion and the high-waisted style of the gown, with a satin bow tied just under her breasts, showcased an impossibly perfect bosom. His chest burned at the way Bellingham's gaze lingered over her curvaceous form. A familiar, intense jolt of dislike for the man hit him anew. He couldn't help wondering if there was any truth to the insinuation the earl had bedded the icy beauty. He couldn't envision it. The bounder wouldn't be present, in the company of Willa's family, if such an outrageous allegation were true. Cam, standing next to Bellingham, caught his eye and waved him over.

"Do join us," he said when Hart neared. "Bellingham, you remember Grey Preston?"

Something hard flickered in Bellingham's eyes when he turned to Hart—likely the memory of the incident during those last days at Cambridge. "Preston," he said in a most droll tone. "How unexpected."

Hart swallowed his distaste. "Bellingham."

Cam's careful gaze shifted between the two. Even he had no idea what had triggered the beating. "Old Grey here has come into the title. He's His Grace now, Duke of Hartwell."

Those steel gray eyes remained carefully empty of expression. "My felicitations."

"Which means Hartwell outranks us all now," Cam continued. If Hart didn't know better, he'd think Cam was needling the earl on purpose. "Quite a switch from the old days, wouldn't you say, Bellingham?"

"Indeed."

Amused, Hart downed his drink. "Cam had little hope for a title and I had no expectation of one of at all." Despite his ambivalence about carrying his brother's title, he could appreciate the irony of their reversed statures. Gus had lorded his high rank over all of them back then. But now, even Cam as a marquess outranked Bellingham.

It seemed to take great effort for Gus to twist his lips into something resembling a smile. "And now you have the greatest of expectations."

After Cam excused himself to greet the newest arrivals, Hart turned to Bellingham. "So Gus, you've finally come into the title that you've coveted for so long."

"Yes." Bellingham's focus shifted back to Willa. "My father's death was a great loss."

"I'm sure you felt it keenly." His eyes followed the same path as Bellingham's. "She's a little out of your depth, wouldn't you say?"

Bellingham's stony gaze returned to Hart. "Beg pardon?"

"Lady Wilhelmina. You aim high."

Bellingham's left brow inched up. He studied Hart with renewed focus, as one might assess a formidable adversary. "You're acquainted with the lady?" The man's tone still suggested disinterest, only now deliberately so.

"She's exceptionally lovely. But considering what I know of your true tastes, I wouldn't think her to be your type."

For an instant, undisguised loathing glowered in Bellingham's eyes. "You know nothing of my tastes." His tone turned easy. "Really, Hartwell, bucks will be bucks. If you're referring to that matter with Erskine, it was a passing amusement and nothing else."

"I doubt Erskine would agree."

"He was weak." Bellingham made a dismissive motion with his hand. "What are you doing here, Hartwell? You are not often out in society."

"Perhaps I am in search of a duchess." Noting the way Bellingham's fingers whitened around his glass, he gave a lazy smile and cast a slow, deliberate look in Willa's direction. "It is well past time I set up a nursery."

Bellingham followed his gaze. "Have a care where you tread, Hartwell. Things are not always as they appear."

"Your continued acceptance in polite society is certainly proof of that."

Bellingham's jaw twitched. "Have you declared yourself to her or made your intentions known to Camryn?"

Hart studied the amber liquid in his glass. "Perhaps I intend to." He took a slow drink. "I can scarcely believe my good fortune that such a rare diamond remains on the marriage mart."

Bright circles of color appeared on each of the earl's cheeks. "Are you certain of that?" Bellingham ground out. "I gather you are not in town much."

"No, I am recently returned from India."

A cold smile. "Of course, I had heard you went to India to find your fortune. Was it to your liking?"

"Enormously so."

"Why am I not surprised a life of trade among savages would suit you."

"If anyone would know about savagery, it would be you." Hart was not ashamed of his business concerns. His considerable fortune was something he'd earned, unlike the dukedom. In many ways, he still thought of his dead brother as the truc Duke of Hartwell. Michael had only been gone for a year and he often still felt like an interloper inhabiting someone else's birthright.

Camryn's butler appeared in the doorway to announce dinner.

"Duty calls. I must escort our hostess in to dinner," Hart said, happy to deliver a tacit reminder that Bellingham ranked well beneath him now. As the highest titled gentleman in the room, it was the duke's duty to escort the dowager marchioness into dinner.

Bellingham bared his teeth in the approximation of a smile. "Of course."

At supper, Hart found himself seated to the marchioness' right with Willa on his other side. Bellingham sat at the opposite end, next to Cam and far from the object of his desire.

Willa did not appear surprised to find herself sitting next to Hartwell. Nor did she seem to mind.

"I find I have the best seat at the table," he said as they took their places.

"Are you certain the air won't be too brisk for you?"

He grinned. "Why Lady Wilhelmina, in your own Arctic way, I do believe you are flirting with me."

"You are our guest," she answered in smooth tones. "Pray don't mistake polite discourse for something that it is not."

"Ouch." He touched his heart in dramatic fashion. Sitting next to her, he'd have no need of dessert. She was like a Gunter's lemon ice—tangy, tart, and delectably frosty.

She curved those pillowed lips into a smile, a reluctant one, but he still counted that a victory. "Surely you are not so easily wounded, Your Grace."

"Actually, as a second son, I have heard far worse. One is not as popular when he is not in line to inherit a dukedom, or at least a vast fortune. As fate would have it, I am now in possession of both."

"Clearly modesty is not something you are in possession of."

Hart gave a mischievous smile. "Usually a title and deep pockets are sufficient to attract the attention of a lovely creature such as yourself." He sipped his wine. "Otherwise, I shall have to win you over with my equally deep reservoirs of charm and good looks."

Her closed mouth wobbled with laughter until she managed to wrangle it into submission. "I should like to know when you decide to begin employing those qualities."

Hart shot her a surprised look. She was teasing him again. Promising. He softened his tone. "Oh, believe me, my lady, I intend to make you well aware of my charms."

Red stung the high planes of her cheeks. "Are you a profligate then," she asked, deliberately setting aside his last words, "who enjoys all of the benefits of a title and none of the responsibilities?"

He grew serious for a moment. "Not at all. I take the responsibilities that matter quite seriously. The running of my estates, ensuring my tenants are treated fairly and have every opportunity to prosper. And I have my business concerns."

"Your sugar trade." When he nodded, she continued. "Do you sell your sugar directly to coffee houses…and other establishments?"

"I do not handle the transactions at that level, but, yes,

my clerks take care of those matters. Do you have an interest in sugar?"

She did not meet his gaze. "Not at all. I was merely making conversation. It is unusual for a gentleman to engage in trade."

"I enjoy enterprise and have little patience for the *ton*'s rules on that matter and on many others, as apparently do you."

"Me?" Willa said in surprise, moving slightly closer to Hart to allow a footman to remove her soup bowl. "Whatever do you mean?"

"The color of your dress, for example. Most eligible young ladies wear white and yet you wear pink this evening. And you are certainly quite eligible." Hart glanced down at her dress, his eyes inadvertently drawn to the enticing swell of her full breasts visible above the neckline. This time even her ears blushed. "I have embarrassed you."

She brought her hands up as if to feel the heat on her cheeks. "Nonsense. It is the curse of my pale complexion that any slight change in temperature can easily be seen in my face."

He gave her a provocative smile. "Have I managed to warm you up, my lady?"

"You are beastly to take pleasure in my discomfort." She smiled ruefully, shaking her head, her gleaming chestnut curls catching the light.

"You mustn't blame me." Her proximity certainly stirred animalistic tendencies in him, especially in the vicinity of his male equipage. "You are an eminently lovely young lady."

She actually snorted. "Not quite so young any longer. However, you have the right of it. I find many of society's dictates trying. If I'm inclined to wear a dress of color, if it is appropriate in its cut, then I should be able to do so without risking the wrath of society." She sipped her wine, leaving a red drop on her full upper lip. Her pink tongue darted out to lick it away. "Besides, one of the advantages of being practically on the shelf is that fewer people are shocked when I choose to wear a bit of color."

"Just a tame pink?" He rolled his eyes over her. "Why not the brightest of reds?"

She laughed, a delightful raspy sound Hart realized he had not heard before. "I didn't say I was fearless. I'm hardly as bold as that. I shudder to think of what it would do to Mother." A mischievous glint touched her eyes. She leaned toward him, inadvertently offering a tantalizing view of full marble-white breasts straining against her bodice. She lowered her voice conspiratorially. "But perhaps one day I shall surprise everyone with a gown of the most vivid color possible. Maybe even a scandalous red."

Hart's heart tugged as the smell of roses taunted his senses. He could easily envision her as a scarlet temptress. Even with her icy demeanor, he was already very much tempted.

. . .

Willa watched the duke wave away a number of meat dishes. He declined both the roast beef and walnut ham before accepting the pigeon pie. There were an awful lot of vegetables on his plate: cabbages, leeks, beets, and parsnips. How unusual. Most men of Willa's acquaintance ate almost nothing but meat.

Hartwell caught her surveying his food choices. His eyes jumped with a hint of heat. "Would you like a taste of my vegetables? They are most succulent."

Willa's ears burned. The man made food sound naughty. "Do you not enjoy the meat dishes? We could have something else prepared."

Hartwell gestured at the array of dishes on the table. There were at least eighteen entrees to choose from. "I could hardly ask for more. I'm afraid my time in India continues to influence my dietary choices."

"You did not eat meat in India?"

Hartwell wiped his mouth and Willa found herself admiring the firm, full curve of his bottom lip. "The Muslims do not eat swine and Hindus forgo the meat of cows."

Willa's ears perked up. "I have read of that. How fascinating."

"Yes, Muslims believe swine is unclean and can harbor disease. It is the Hindu belief that cows contain hundreds of deities."

Willa's eyes widened. "They believe cows are God-like?"

"Do you suppose that is where the expression 'holy cow' came from?"

She'd never heard that expression. "How peculiar and intriguing that some people believe in the sanctity of cows."

"So you can understand my reluctance to eat beef while I was there." He leaned back in his chair. "It seemed somewhat rude. Over time, I simply lost a taste for it."

"Remarkable," Willa said, shaking her head in wonder. "The world is truly full of fascinating people and customs." She looked around the table, feeling a keen pang of longing. "Someday I hope to see all of it for myself." She realized

Hartwell had stopped eating to fix a dark penetrating gaze on her. She flushed. "I'm sure you think me a silly dreamer."

"Not at all." His eyes shone with an intensity which belied his light tone. She felt the impact of that look deep into her stomach. "I was just thinking of how fortunate a man would be to have you look at him with that same kind of enthusiasm."

"Lady Wilhelmina." The portly older man seated on her other side held up a meat pastry. "Perhaps you can solve the mystery of whether this is pigeon or chicken. I say pigeon but Charles here insists it is chicken."

"Why, I believe Cook mixed the two meats for a more flavorful outcome, Mr. Magee." She had no idea what kind of meat it was yet she turned toward the older man, grateful to get out from under Hartwell's intense gaze. Out of the corner of her eye, she saw the duke turn his attention to Lady Joanna Rawdon, a vivacious widow with black hair and a slender frame who sat opposite him.

Magee took another bite of his pastry. "Hmmm. Yes, now there's an intriguing thought." Willa nodded her head, pretending to listen, while her mind lingered on Hartwell. She remained aware of the duke's movements when he gave a light laugh or took another drink.

He looked incredibly appealing in his formal clothes. Impeccable as usual, his breeches, waistcoat, and jacket were all black. His blinding white cravat shone against his jet-black hair, tied neatly back. She wondered how Hartwell would look with his hair down. What would it feel like to run her fingers through those thick black strands? Warmth stirred inside her stomach. Trying to change the direction of her thoughts, she looked away, inadvertently locking eyes with Augustus at the opposite end of the dining table, who did nothing to disguise the fact that he was watching her.

"Do you plan to eventually accept his suit?"

She blinked at Hartwell. "I beg your pardon?" She realized he'd followed her gaze down the length of the table.

"Your earl? Bellingham."

She cast him a searing look. "He is not 'my' anything, as you well know."

"He does not appear at all aware of that. The fop has not taken his eyes off of you throughout the entire meal."

If she didn't know better, she'd think Hartwell was jealous. A burst of pleasure shot through her. "What exactly is between the two of you?"

"I must say your sister's betrothal was a surprise," he said, changing the subject. "A rather interesting development, all things considered. I had not seen an announcement."

"There wasn't one," Willa answered. "It would be inappropriate since the old earl died so recently. The betrothal and wedding are to be quiet affairs. Race and Adela are keen to marry quickly, but they must wait for the mourning period to end."

"I thought his Christian name was Horace."

"Race is a nickname we all gave him years ago." She smiled at the memory. "He was the fastest of runners. Race could outpace anyone, win any challenge."

"Race, ah, hence the nickname."

He followed Willa's gaze down the table to where the betrothed couple sat side by side. Race seemed oblivious to all of them. His head tilted toward his smiling future bride as he talked intently to her. Addie's eyes were riveted on her betrothed. "A proverbial love match?"

Willa smiled, eyeing the couple. "Oh, yes. They grew up together just as—" Just as she and Augustus had. But Willa stopped herself before saying it out loud. She cleared her throat. "They knew each other growing up and developed an attachment that continues to this day."

She felt Hartwell's inscrutable eyes on her. The intensity of that dark look made Willa uneasy. The duke appeared quiet and distracted as the footmen came to remove the tablecloth to prepare for dessert. Then he turned again to Joanna Rawdon, the lovely widow across the table, and began chatting with her.

• • •

Cam sat back in his chair and took a long drink. The ladies had retired to the salon, leaving the men to their port. "So Bellingham, I hear you've taken up quite a bet at White's."

Bellingham raised a glass in salute. "Ten thousand guineas says McPherson beats Abbott in the ring." The younger brother shifted in his seat, drawing Hartwell's attention. Horace Manning's jaw worked. He seemed angry.

David Selwyn let out a low whistle. "Ten thousand guineas on a boxing match?" He shook his head. "You are either brave or careless, my friend. Perhaps both."

"Yes, perhaps both," mumbled the brother.

Cam bottomed out his glass. "I don't think I've ever met a more prolific betting man. It's a fortunate thing you have an earldom to support your gaming habits."

Bellingham nodded and proceeded to relieve himself at the table with a chamber pot. Hart averted his eyes with distaste. Englishmen thought the Indians were barbarians, but at least they never pissed where they ate.

Bellingham tucked his flaccid member back into his breeches while a footman hurried away with the chamber pot. "Indeed, and a very profitable one at that." He looked pointedly at Hartwell. "Although, of course, I don't bother myself with the dreary financial details."

The man really was an idiot. Hartwell took a long drag on his cheroot, exhaling silvery circles that dissipated into nothingness.

Afterwards, the men rejoined the women in the salon. The room had grown warmer, so the doors leading to the garden were thrown open, allowing cooler air to circulate. Hart paused by the door. He looked out into the garden, taking in the light cool breeze.

The widow appeared at his side. She snapped open her fan, peeking over it in a practiced flirtatious manner. Joanna Rawdon was a perky thing, with saucy little breasts on full display. She batted her eyelashes. "Do you see anything you like, Your Grace?"

She obviously wasn't referring to anything in the garden. "I am ever appreciative of nature's bounty," he said with practiced gallantry.

Her eyelashes fluttered. "I too appreciate nature's beauty."

"I say, Lady Rawdon, what is your opinion? Was it pigeon or chicken in those delectable pastries?" asked Magee joining them, apparently having been unable to resolve the issue at the supper table. "Perhaps I should have another taste." From the way the old codger eyed the widow's breasts, the meat pastries weren't the only things he wanted to taste.

"I'm sure I don't know," Lady Rawdon replied in a bored tone, looking disappointed to have her tête à tête with Hart disturbed. Not that Hart minded. Another time, he might have appreciated what the lady had to offer. This evening, however, his focus remained fastened on a certain lady with luscious curves and a tart little tongue he wouldn't mind tasting. Where had she gone?

As if his thoughts had summoned her, Hart felt a light tap on his arm and turned to find Willa smiling up at him, a little flush high on her cheeks. Was she actually batting her eyelashes at him?

"Your Grace. I find I am a little overheated. Would you be so kind as to accompany me outside?" She offered him her hand.

The cool princess actively seeking his company? Up until this moment, Willa had treated him with what could best be described as friendly contempt. How much wine had she had at supper? Perhaps there was hope for the frosty female after all.

"Of course, it would be my pleasure." Offering his arm, he sketched a quick bow to Magee and Lady Rawdon, and ignored the petulant look the widow threw him. They strolled outside where Willa took a seat on the ledge of the modest fountain that dominated much of the small garden.

Taking a spot beside her, Hart smiled. "Dare I hope your feelings toward me have warmed?"

"Beg pardon?" She seemed distracted. Her eyes darted toward the salon's open doors. "Did you enjoy the meal?"

The small ray of warmth he'd glimpsed just a moment ago vanished again, her veiled façade firmly back in place. "Yes, though I assume it is your mother, and perhaps

Camryn, I should thank for my invitation."

She didn't say anything to that. Hart let his eyes rest on her for a moment, taking in the way the moonlight danced over the defined slopes of her perfect face, down the elegant turn of neck. Desire curled through him.

The lady seemed aware of the change in him because a luminous smile lit up her face. She focused her full attention on him, leaning toward him, putting her hand on his arm in a daring fashion. She tilted her face upward almost as though inviting a kiss.

His rod leapt to attention. What the devil? She pursed those full inviting lips of hers. Her luscious pale bosom—almost bursting out of her gown—actually heaved in his direction. Good lord, the woman was a glistening bundle of temptation. Hot lust unfurled deep in his belly. He leaned in, intent on feeling those delectable lips under his own.

And then she spoke.

"Oh, Your Grace," she simmered. Hart frowned. It was not at all her usual tone. And she appeared a little too breathless for a woman as sensible as he knew her to be. Her eyes darted toward the salon again where someone rustled in the doorway. Hart turned just in time to make out Bellingham retreating from the threshold.

Irritation rifled through him, even as disappointment hollowed his belly. Had the lady staged this little show of false affection for Bellingham's benefit? To what end?

She pulled back the minute Bellingham disappeared inside, relief etched in the lovely lines of her face. But the game wasn't quite over yet. She'd practically asked for a kiss and he would make sure she got one.

He leaned in, slipping his hand around Willa's waist

to ease her toward him. He'd never kissed a gently born innocent before. Assuming, of course, she was still a maiden. Normally, his instinct would be to give her a quick brush on the lips. Instead, he covered her lips with his in a kiss that was both gentle and insistent, intent on giving her a true taste of passion. She gasped against his mouth and his blood boiled at the feel of her hands coming flat against his chest as though she meant to push him away.

To his satisfaction, she gave up the fight immediately and her body softened into his. Supple, pillowed lips pressed back against his, inviting him to take more. The lavish curves of her body nestled against the hard lines of his, their plush softness enveloping him, the smell of roses searing his man's flesh. She became even more pliant in his arms, and triumph surged through him when Willa parted her mouth to take him in. As soon as he felt her sensual acquiescence, he forced himself to release her, lest he take her right here in the garden.

Willa's eyes flew open. She looked stunned and then immediately disappointed, her body still trembling from his kiss. A baser part of him took dark pleasure in seeing how his touch affected her.

She blinked. "What was that?"

He struggled to regulate his harsh breaths. "Such fire you have, beneath that ice."

"You kissed me," she said blankly.

He couldn't abide the idea of her going to Bellingham. "I thought you should have a real taste of passion before attaching yourself to that cold fish."

She frowned. "Whatever do you mean?"

"Bellingham." He struggled to keep his tone even,

despite the uproar kissing her had incited within his body. "You did stage this little show for his benefit, did you not? Perhaps you hope to inspire jealousy."

She recoiled. "How dare you?"

Heat and lust pounded through his heart deep down into his gut. "You so clearly wanted to be kissed. I merely obliged."

Shaking, she jumped to her feet, her hands clenched into fists at her sides. "To take such advances and then to act like a…like a cad! To treat me like a common—"

Forcing his gaze away from her swollen lips, Hart pushed to his feet. "Like a common what?" His words dripped with sarcasm. "I merely gave the lady what she desired. Was it not to your liking? Perhaps you would care to make another attempt. Or maybe not, since we don't have an audience."

She gasped at the realization he'd seen Augustus in the doorway. "You pressed your advances on me even though you knew I was not serious? You took grievous advantage of me, sir!"

"I took advantage of you?" He moved his face near to hers, his soft tone laced with contempt. "Do you know what one calls a lady who seeks advances from a man in front of an appreciative audience?" He didn't wait for her answer. Jealousy dimmed his vision and the angry words careened off his tongue. "I can tell you such women are not usually found in Mayfair and, I assure you, we do not call them 'ladies.'"

Her hand lashed out to slap him, but he caught her by the wrist, his eyes never leaving her face. Their bodies almost touching, she radiated heat, and her breath rasped out in short, quick pants. Her eyes gleamed with outrage and something else so blatantly sensual, it was all he could do not to toss her to the ground and take her right there.

Struggling for control, he said, "In the future, do not play games that you are unwilling to see to completion."

She yanked her wrist out of his grip and smoothed any emotion out of her face. "I suspect you play an altogether different game, one that began at Cambridge." Each wintry word scraped against his heated skin like an icy shard. "Your animus toward the earl is well known and I have no intention of being a weapon in your battle with him."

The magnificent ice queen was returned. He uttered a contemptuous laugh. "Strange. I thought I was the pawn this evening. And you the puppet master."

"If only." She drew back her shoulders, straightened her spine, and glided back into the drawing room.

Chapter Six

Two weeks later, Hart met with the merchant whose property he hoped to purchase for his London headquarters. They conducted their meeting at the three-story building on Bond Street, which housed a coffee house on the street level.

Simple in design, the coffee house was a comfortable and welcoming place, furnished mostly with tables and chairs although a few larger, more comfortable seats were clustered around the hearth. A young boy of perhaps eleven cleared the tables, but Hart noted that most of the employees were women.

"Who manages this establishment?" he asked Mr. Webb, the building's current owner.

"A Mr. Gordon, Your Grace. Although I have never had the pleasure of making the gentleman's acquaintance." Webb led the way up the stairs. "He lives abroad and the rent arrives regularly from a solicitor here in Town."

"I see mostly females work here."

"Yes, he's a bit of a radical, our Mr. Gordon. He employs widows who have fallen into dire straits." Leaning closer to Hart, he lowered his voice. "Although I do suspect some of these wenches have never had a husband, if you take my meaning. I've increased the rent twice to encourage their decampment, but to no avail."

After a tour of the upstairs space, Hart determined it would be adequate for his needs and told Webb to expect further correspondence from his man of business. Once the meeting concluded, he spotted Cam arriving at the coffee house with David Selwyn, their old friend from Cambridge.

"Hart, it is good to find you here," the marquess said amiably. "Won't you join us?" He'd seen Cam several times over the course of the last couple of weeks, their friendship picking up where it had left off before Hart went to India. They'd met up at the gaming tables, or at Brooks, and had taken in a boxing match.

There was no mention of Willa, even though she'd taken up permanent residence inside Hart's mind; both that toe-curling kiss and his own regrettable behavior afterward. His words had been reprehensible. Cruel even. He'd not intended to allude to her already-damaged reputation, but his temper had gotten the better of him. It struck him that he was driven by jealousy. Provoked by an oaf like Bellingham, of all people, thanks to an infuriating, incomparable chit with intelligent eyes, a tart tongue, and endless curves.

He'd immediately tried to apologize to the lady for his base behavior, yet the flowers he'd sent the following morning had been returned, as was the contrite note that followed. All refused in a manner which provoked reluctant admiration in him. Few females rejected the persistent attentions of a duke.

Agreeing to join his friends, Hart asked, "Do you frequent this establishment?" He wondered if they would miss the coffee house should he force its closure, which seemed likely. He needed the space for his clerks.

"It is my first visit, but Willa has recently discovered it and can't stop talking about the tea." Cam gestured toward a table by the window. "The ladies are already seated. We were to meet them here once they'd completed their shopping."

The mention of Willa prickled his insides. He followed Cam's gaze to find the lady in question sitting with her sister and a slender girl with outlandishly red hair. "Look who we've run into," Cam said as the men joined the ladies. He turned to Willa. "You missed Bellingham again. He came to call as I departed to join you here."

The sister perked up. "Was Race with him?"

Cam chucked her playfully on the chin. "No, you little hoyden. However, I understand he is joining us this evening for supper." Hart barely heard the interaction. So Bellingham had taken to calling upon Willa with some regularity. Irritation flicked his chest.

"It is to our great fortune to join you ladies," said Selwyn.

Willa favored Selwyn with a soft smile, and those luminous eyes glistened. "Are you always so gallant, Mr. Selwyn?" Selwyn flushed, almost imperceptibly, but he was clearly not immune to the attentions of a beautiful lady. What male wouldn't react to her?

"What is good here?" Hart asked almost gruffly. "I understand you favor this establishment, Lady Wilhelmina."

Cool chocolate eyes moved to him with obvious reluctance, all warmth gone from them. She looked unbelievably alluring in a soft lavender robe with delicate golden embroidery that also trimmed her matching turban. "The tea blends here are quite excellent."

"Coffee for me." Cam winked at his cousin. "All tea is bland next to Willa's."

She smiled at the flattery, an honest reaction, radiant and unencumbered, buoyed by her obvious affection for Camryn. The redhead who'd been introduced as Lady Florinda gave an impish smile. "Perhaps you should try it, my lord. The tea here is without equal—with the exception of Willa's, of course."

Willa fixed the girl with a quelling look. "Let Cam have his coffee, Flor."

What was that about? Perhaps the lady worried her blends would pale in comparison to the establishment's tea. Having sampled Willa's exceptional tea, he doubted that could happen. "I should like some tea," he said.

"This is not the usual coffee house," Hart commented once they had all placed their orders.

"Mostly women work here, Your Grace," the redhead answered with a vivacious smile. "Women do have a right to support their families." Her tone almost dared him to disagree. Hart bit back a smile. Red would be a handful for any future husband.

"That is most commendable," said Selwyn. "Who is the proprietor?"

"He is said to live abroad," Hart said, giving Willa a sidelong glance. Those plush lips were pushed together in a mutinous line. Lord, but she was a beauty, one who seemed determined to engage him as little as possible. "Do you have any knowledge of the owner, Lady Wilhelmina?"

She gave a slow, deliberate blink as though it pained her to respond. "You appear to be acquainted with him. Was that not the owner of the building we saw you with just now?"

"Mr. Webb. Yes, I have business with him, but he does not own the coffee house enterprise."

"I only know it is a respectable establishment where a lady might meet with her acquaintances without fear of censure."

He looked at the books on the table. "You read here as well?"

"Our Ladies Reading Society meets here from time to time," said Red.

"That is most unusual. Meeting in a public place."

Willa smiled insincerely, as cool and polite as ever. "Perhaps you are not accustomed to ladies who read."

He ignored the provocation. "May I ask what you are reading?"

She cut him a defiant glance. "*A Vindication of the Rights of Woman*."

"Ah, Mary Wollstonecraft then."

Her eyes widened. "You are familiar with her?"

"Perhaps not as much as you, but I am aware of some of her…ah…themes."

The sister, who had appeared quite bored, straightened up. "A vindication of what? I thought you were reading one of those Maria Edgeworth novels."

"Mary Wollstonecraft's *A Vindication of the Rights of Woman*. It's a treatise on the rights of women," she said to her sister before returning Hart's unwavering gaze. "Frankly, I'm surprised the Duke of Hartwell would read such a forward-thinking document."

"I do pick up a book on occasion. I hear it exercises the mind."

Ignoring his sarcasm, Willa perched her chin on her hand, regarding him with renewed interest. "And what do you think?"

"Well, in the defense of my gender, I hardly think it is the fault of men that women are regarded as objects of allure. They are objects of allure. Pure and simple." He tried not to stare at her pink lips or to become too entranced by the luxurious chocolate of her enormous eyes. "It is the way of nature. Men and women are supposed to attract each other. That attraction is vital…er…to the perpetuation of the human race."

Willa leaned forward and the smell of roses slinked around him, making it difficult to think. "But you are purposely focusing your attention on only one side of Miss Wollstonecraft's argument," she said. "Gentlemen are allowed to enjoy and even act upon that attraction to women of all sorts. But you are also free to pursue many other interests. As a woman, I am not. I am to keep to home and hearth."

The sister rolled her eyes. "Willa, His Grace will think you are quite radical when nothing could be further from the truth."

Hartwell smiled at Lady Adela. "Not at all, my lady. I find the discourse most engaging." He turned his attention back to Willa. "Pray do continue, Lady Wilhelmina."

"A woman is entitled to more than a domestic education. If a woman has no interest in domestic pursuits, she is doomed to a life of boredom," Willa said. "Her mind is essentially wasted."

"Some would argue that women do have a duty," said Selwyn, still obviously dazzled by Willa's radiance. "The importance of raising a family and running a household are not to be underestimated."

"But what if a woman does not marry?" she said. "At my age, I will likely never marry. Am I doomed, then, to a life without intellectual pursuit?"

The lady's eyes glittered with activity, a lovely flush of color high on her cheeks. Hart had never seen her so animated and engaged, her aloof demeanor stripped away, her passion apparent. Ah, to have that passion directed at oneself. "Is that what you desire, the right to never marry?"

"Yes. I shall never wed." Willa's answer was firm. "But if I were to marry and bear children, wouldn't they be best served by a mother who is educated? Should they not be guided by a mother with an active, learned mind? An educated woman is best for her family and for society. So it follows that educated women are good for the prosperity of the nation."

Hart had always liked women with keen minds. But social debates had never aroused both his mind and body before. By God, this unwitting temptress had his blood surging through his body in mindless anticipation.

"I concur with that part of Miss Wollstonecraft's argument," he said. "A well-educated woman is an asset not only to herself, but to her husband and children. And, of course, that benefits a civilized society. It is my contention, though, that members of your gender can be alluring to men as well as highly educated and intelligent. The two are not necessarily mutually exclusive."

The arrival of the tea interrupted their discussion. Sipping it, Hart realized the brew not only compared to Willa's, it actually surpassed it. In fact, the hint of citrus combined with an edge of rosemary sweetened with cinnamon was frisky on the tongue in a way that might make it the best cup of tea he'd ever had.

He looked up to find Willa watching him with more than just a passing curiosity. In fact, that intense, almost anticipatory look was remarkably similar to the one she'd worn the day he'd tasted her tea at Camryn House. Come to think of it, this tea seemed quite similar to that tea. Too similar. As though it had in fact been mixed by the same hand.

His eyebrows lifted. Surely she wouldn't dare sell her blends. No lady would court scandal like that, not even one who spouted the virtues of Wollstonecraft. "This tea is quite good actually, excellent even."

Her answering smile of satisfaction told him all he needed to know. "Yes," she said in a propriety manner. "It is why Flor and I frequent this establishment."

"It tastes familiar somehow."

Willa's expression froze with her lush lips slightly parted. Red sputtered into her teacup and coughed several times.

"Lady Florinda?" Cam leaned forward to offer her his kerchief. "Are you well?"

"Yes, quite well," Red choked out, her face as flaming as her hair. She grabbed the linen cloth and put it to her mouth. "Thank you ever so much."

Hart downed more tea. "Yes, I'm sure of it. Do you agree the tea tastes familiar, Lady Wilhelmina?"

Steely eyes met his. "I can't say that it does."

"Really?" Taking another sip, he allowed the warm

liquid to roll around in his mouth. "Of course, your blends are sharper on the tongue."

"Flor is unwell." She pushed to her feet quite abruptly, added color tingeing those high cheekbones. Sadly, he couldn't check the temperature of her ears because they were hidden beneath her turban. "We should go."

"Are you certain?" he said as the gentlemen came to their feet. "We were having such an enlightening conversation."

"Yes." She gave him a frigid look. "Quite sure."

After a moment's delay, Red got to her feet. "I do feel rather badly."

"You are a bit flushed," he said, amusement in his voice. "Allow me to see you home."

Willa's enormous eyes narrowed. "That will not be necessary. Cam can escort us."

"I suppose Selwyn and I will stay behind to finish our tea." Hart bowed. "What did you say this blend is called?"

"I didn't say." Taking Red by the arm, she smiled serenely, not about to get caught in his obvious trap. "Come, Florinda, let us go."

Looking back over her shoulder as Willa firmly guided her away, Red called back to him, "It's called Heavenly Tea."

• • •

Willa moved about the morning room mixing her latest tea blend for the shop when Smythe appeared with a sizeable package.

"Who is it from?" she asked, eyeing the parcel.

"It was just delivered by a footman in the Duke of Hartwell's livery."

A pang cramped Willa's insides, a mix of both ire and lingering wounded feelings after his humiliation of her in the garden. She turned back to her tea leaves. "Send it back."

"I am to read the accompanying note to you before the parcel is returned."

"That won't be necessary." Willa measured out the leaves. "I'm not the least bit interested."

Smythe cleared his throat. "Please, my lady, I wouldn't want His Grace displeased with me. And if her ladyship learns of this—"

She regretted the butler's distress. He'd had to rebuff both an earl and a duke on her behalf more than once this week. She shook her head with exasperation. It was as though everyone had suddenly forgotten she was ruined.

Without turning around, she said, "Oh, very well, just read it and have done with it."

"Yes, my lady." Relief weighted his voice. "If I may, it says, 'To an angel of a lady who mixes the most heavenly of teas.'"

The silver mixing spoon clattered to the floor. She whirled around. "What else does it say?"

"That is all," he said serenely. "Shall I return the package now?"

So Hartwell had rightly guessed the coffee house tea was her very own blend. Icy fear gave way to a rising tide of indignation. Did he mean to threaten her into accepting his notes and gifts? "You may leave the parcel. That will be all."

After Smythe departed, Willa eyed the sizable package. A fiery sensation flared in her chest at the thought of Hartwell. And that kiss. Passionate and delicious in a way that made her insides clamor for more, Hartwell's embrace had been nothing like her regrettable intimacy with Augustus. She'd never willingly opened her mouth for Augustus; it had disgusted her. Yet, with Hartwell, her lips had parted almost of their own volition. She'd *wanted* to taste him.

And then he'd stopped. With the harsh words that followed, her humiliation had been complete. Rumors of her ruination had undoubtedly reached him. Why else would he have treated her like a strumpet? She had only herself to blame for the soreness in her chest when she thought of the duke; she of all people shouldn't require reminders about the true nature of men. Besides, Hartwell's meeting with Mr. Webb suggested he was the potential buyer who meant to purchase the building and close the coffee house. Clearly, it meant nothing to the duke to put struggling mothers out of work.

Staring at the package now, her first instinct was to throw it out since she couldn't send it back but — drat it all — curiosity finally got the better of her. She untied the string binding it and something fluttered to the floor. Another note. She stooped to pick it up. The words were written with a heavy hand in sharp, decisive strokes — not unlike the man who'd wielded the pen.

Forgive the tactics but my apology is most sincere.

Sincere. She knew a thing or two about men and their sincerity. Her father had professed his devotion to her mother but that hadn't kept him from straying. And hadn't Augustus pledged his undying regard for her? Her attention returned to the package. She could still throw it out. If only she wasn't so curious to learn what it contained.

She tore away the paper to reveal some sort of wooden box. Her breath caught as the most exquisite tea caddy she'd ever seen came into full view. The rich scent of dark wood and something faintly exotic drifted into the air. She stared at the intricate swirls of design which was inlaid with both brass and smooth ivory. It was perhaps the most beautiful object she'd ever seen.

Admiring the molded edges, she released the clasp to lift the finely crafted, stepped lid. Inside, the triple caddy contained two glass jars and a bowl. Her eyes widened. The glass jars were filled with tea, but nothing she recognized. Opening one of them, she inhaled a singular musky spiciness that sent her senses swirling. What was it? Closing her eyes, she took in the deep, rich, earthy fragrance again. This tea would be sweet, perhaps malty. Was it from India? She had to taste it. Ringing for Smythe, she asked for tea to be sent up right away.

While she waited, she ran her fingers along the cool dark wood of the tea caddy and her thoughts returned to Hartwell. She smiled, reluctantly admiring his clever gift. He barely knew her, yet this gift suggested otherwise, for he'd selected the one thing in this world she could never bring herself to return. But it didn't mean she'd forgiven him. And she certainly didn't trust his intentions any more today than she had yesterday.

• • •

The following afternoon, Willa set out for the coffee house with her latest blend tucked under one arm. She was in a hurry because the last package she'd sent over had been misplaced. Pamela's footman swore he'd delivered it, but the women at the shop could not seem to place it.

The timing couldn't have been worse. Lady Rawdon, the lovely widow who had an eye for Hartwell, had scheduled a gathering at the coffee house today. The anticipated profits would pay the establishment's expenses, including the workers' wages, for a month.

Too impatient to wait in the front hall for the carriage to be brought around, she stepped out onto the sidewalk and her heart sank when an opulent coach-and-four bearing the Bellingham insignia pulled up.

A Bellingham footman jumped down from his place at the back of the horse-drawn carriage to open the door. Augustus' chiseled profile leaned into view. "The lovely Lady Wilhelmina." He eyed her package. "Are you going somewhere? Allow me to convey you there."

She looked around. Where was her carriage? Time was running short. Lady Rawdon's event would commence at any moment. She had to get the tea there in time. "Very well. It will be just a moment for my abigail."

Augustus extended a hand to help her up into the coach. "No need for that." A cool smile. "After all, we are practically family."

She stood her ground well away from the coach. As if she would ever place herself in a position of vulnerability with him again. "I go nowhere without Clara."

A footman hurried inside to call for Willa's maid. Only when she finally rushed out, pulling on her bonnet, did Willa allow the earl to hand her up into his coach. Clara slipped in beside her. Augustus took the seat opposite them, his back to the driver. He tapped on the roof, signaling the coachman to drive on.

"I am going to the coffee house on Bond Street," Willa

said. "Do you know it?"

His brow arched. "I do indeed. Although I have to say it is distasteful the way unchaperoned innocents have taken to congregating there."

Glancing out the window, she wished the coachman would move faster. "It is a perfectly respectable establishment."

"I should like to announce our betrothal immediately."

She swung her head from the window to him. "I am not marrying you. I've made myself quite clear in that regard."

"I should think your reputation would not allow you to be so choosy."

"Whose fault is it that my reputation is not as pristine as it once was?" she retorted while Clara shifted uncomfortably beside her.

"Exactly." He regarded her over the bridge of his well-formed nose. "I am most willing to rectify it."

She shook her head, thoroughly exasperated. "I do not wish to marry. Not you nor anyone else." The carriage lurched to a halt. "Why have we stopped?"

"London traffic is atrocious." His austere expression chilled. "Perhaps you await your duke."

"He is not my duke. I don't know what this feud between you and Hartwell is about, but I want nothing to do with it."

"Impossible. You are the prize we both intend to claim."

"Please. Hartwell has no serious interest in me." She almost laughed at the irony. For years, there had been no suitors save a bevy of fortune hunters. And now both a duke and an earl vied for her attention? "I'm quite the tainted prize, wouldn't you say?"

His expression firmed. "I don't intend to lose to that man."

The carriage inched forward. She regarded Augustus with open curiosity, taking in the sun-shot curls and high-cut cheekbones. Without a doubt, he was pleasingly formed, probably the most handsome man of her acquaintance, yet his presence now left her completely unmoved.

"Why did Hartwell pummel you at university?" she asked.

"Isn't it obvious?" If her question surprised him, he gave no sign of it. "I was the heir and he a second son with few prospects. I was deep in my cups which gave him quite an advantage during that unfortunate encounter."

The carriage stopped again. Willa glanced out of the window. She would be late to the coffee house if they didn't start moving again soon. She turned her attention back to Augustus. "But that was long ago and now he is a duke. Why would the animus linger?"

"Hartwell has always wanted what I have." His lips twisted into an ironic smile. "Claiming you would be his ultimate revenge. The entire metropolis knows I intend to have you. Hartwell was aware of it even at university."

"Beg pardon? That was years ago."

"As your cousin's particular friend, it was well known to him I planned to return home to pledge my troth to you."

Disappointment contracted her stomach. Now it all made sense—the flowers, the ride in the park, the incredible tea caddy—all calculated to win her so Hartwell might claim his final triumph over Augustus. None of it had been done out of a real desire to court her.

The carriage jerked to a stop again. Feeling stifled, Willa had to get away. She unlatched the door and jumped out into the crowded street.

Bellingham's brows rose. "Get back inside here," he demanded from the window. "You cannot walk on a London street alone. Have you taken leave of your senses?"

When Clara moved to follow Willa, Augustus fixed a glare on her. "Be still," he snapped. "Your mistress is not going anywhere."

His high-handed manner grated Willa's nerves. "Oh, yes I am. Clara, come."

The earl placed his arm across the coach's open door, blocking the maid's exit. "I command you to stay seated."

Clearly cowed, Clara cast a desperate look at Willa. "Please, my lady."

Furious at his intimidation of her maid, Willa turned away. "Do not worry, Clara. I'm sure his lordship will drop you at home. I'm late. Walking will be faster." She tucked the tea package under her arm and started in the direction of Bond Street. "Good day. I shall see myself to the coffee house."

"Come back here." His voice growing angrier, he alighted to follow her. "You cannot walk unaccompanied."

Irritated, but also well aware that he had the right of it, Willa slowed to allow the earl to catch up. It was folly to walk alone on the street. His footman followed at a discreet distance.

"You have never had any sense when it comes to guarding your virtue," he said as he approached.

Anger burned in her stomach. "Yes, one never knows when a cad will take liberties with an innocent girl." High handed lummox. She had to escape his company. Weaving through the mass of people, she hurried along, anxious to lose her determined escort.

"Willa," he called, gaining on her.

She rushed to beat a costermonger who slowly pushed his cart along. Augustus got trapped behind the man. She made her way through the masses, sidestepping the throng of people to avoid being jostled. Her heart thumping, she ignored Augustus' calls and forced herself not to look back. She didn't slow her gait even after she lost the earl somewhere far back behind her.

She had never walked alone in Town. If Mother learned of this, she'd never hear the end of it. But she was as good as ruined and never intended to marry anyway, so she may as well enjoy experiencing the world on her own terms. Exhaling, she slowed to take in the scene around her. Fruit sellers called out, advertising their wares. The carts and drays jostled for a lane. People hurried along with their purchases.

A small boy stepped in front of Willa, startling her. "Flowers, my lady?" He pushed a bouquet up to her. Smiling and without breaking her stride, Willa reached into her reticule and tossed him a coin. A huge grin lit the unwashed boy's face as she moved on, leaving him with both the blunt and his flowers. Turning away from the child, she halted when a dray with a heavy load stopped in front of her. She stepped around it just as the cart lurched forward.

Willa's pulse hammered at the thought of being out alone among this human traffic. Yet it felt freeing, exhilarating even, to be on her own in this way, seizing control of this small sliver of her life. Even the malodorous smell of sewage, unwashed people, and rotting fruit did little to hamper her quiet joy.

Forcing herself to breathe evenly, Willa ducked into an alley which provided a shortcut to the backside of the coffee house so she would not be seen entering alone. Hugging the tea to her chest, she maintained a determined stride. Just a little ways more and she would be there.

Something rustled behind her. Willa's breath hitched and she quickened her pace. It was probably just a rat. Another swish sounded even closer behind her. Trying to convince herself it must be a very large rodent, Willa did not turn around. She had the rear of the coffee house in her sights now. A few more steps and she would be there. Footsteps pounded close behind, gaining on her. It was no rat. At least not the four-legged kind. Willa sprinted toward the coffee house.

Someone grabbed her arm. She screamed and tried to snatch it away. Her assailant's grasp firmed as he slammed her front-first up against the rough wall of the building next to the coffee house, knocking the breath out of her. Heart pumping, she struggled in vain as his unyielding body pressed hers firmly against the wall. He made a sound of appreciation and something much more primal. Fear clawed her insides. He wrenched her wrists high above her head while his other hand reached around to fondle her breast before ripping her bodice, tearing away the delicate fabric of her chemise.

She choked out a cry when he jerked her wrists higher over her head, the jolting pain tearing at her armpits. She struggled against his superior strength, desperate to wrest her arms loose, her panic growing when she registered his arousal firming against the small of her back.

Her mind working furiously, she forced a sob and deliberately went limp against him. Throwing him off guard was her only hope of escape. "Please don't."

"You're wanting it," he panted against her neck, speaking in a voice that sounded surprisingly polished for a common footpad. He smelled of masculine exertion, but otherwise did not carry the unwashed odor of the streets. "I plan to give it to you until you're screaming for more. You're a fine piece."

But he relaxed his hold a bit, clearly believing she'd given in. She had to act now. Girding herself, she jerked her head forward and slammed it back with as much force as she could muster, the movement followed by the sickening crack of his nose.

"Arg!" He jerked away. "You bitch!"

Her arms free, she spun away without giving him another look and raced blindly toward the coffee house. The sound of footsteps pounded behind her, gaining ground. A firm hand closed around her arm. She spun around with flailing arms, panicked, but also angry and defiant, determined to fight him off. "Get away from me, you lout!"

Strong gentle hands grasped her wrists, stopping them from pummeling him. "Willa, it is me. Hartwell. Look at me."

The second her mind registered the words, Willa's knees gave way and she sank into the warm safety of his body. His steady arms lifted her against his hard chest. She clasped his neck, burrowing her face in his shoulder, soaking up the scent of soap and cheroots, the comforting fragrance that was uniquely him.

"What is that commotion?" a voice said from the vicinity of the coffee house.

"Damnation." Hart cursed under his breath and ducked into the back door of the building.

"Who was it?" she managed to croak.

"Joanna Rawdon. The lady has a tongue that won't stop flapping."

Willa groaned. To be seen now was to assure her complete and total ruination. Forever. They entered the kitchen. The workers paused to gape at the duke with the disheveled woman in his arms.

"Is there a place of privacy?" Hart asked in a commanding tone. It must have been his duke voice, stern and unrelenting. She had never heard it before now.

A young girl showed them into a storeroom with a pallet for a bed in the corner. Three chairs were gathered around a small table. Crates of stores were stacked up against every wall. Hart kicked the door shut behind them. He put her down, but kept a firm grasp of her elbows to give her strength to stand.

Concern pooled in his deep blue eyes. "Are you well? Should I send for Camryn?" His gaze slipped to her torn bodice. "Or a physician?" he asked in a soft voice.

She sank against his chest. "No, no. He didn't truly harm me. I'm shaken up more than anything."

His arms closed around her in a warm cocoon. "I feared the worst when I saw you, with your gown torn and your hair—" A gentle hand tilted her chin upward until she looked into the midnight blue of his eyes. Profound tenderness marked his face, gentling the sharpness of his features. "Are you certain he didn't…abuse you?"

"No, of course not." She felt a pang of emotion at the caring protectiveness in his voice. "I managed to fight him off. He is probably more injured than I."

He chuckled softly. "Why does that not surprise me?"

"How did you come to be here?"

"Cam and I met here to take tea. I slipped out to have a cheroot since I could not partake in the presence of ladies. There seems to be some event taking place."

She'd forgotten. "Lady Rawdon's tea." The widow must have arrived early to ensure that everything had been properly arranged. "Thank you for coming to my rescue." Without thinking, she instinctively leaned further into the warmth of his arms. She knew it was inappropriate, but she didn't care. He made her feel protected and at the moment, there was nothing she needed more than this safe harbor. She closed her arms around his waist, pressing her body closer to his, buoyed by his heated strength.

He hesitated at first, but then seemed to understand. His arms tightened around her, the full length of her body snuggled against the hard curves of his, the clean scent of him embracing her. Hart dropped a soft kiss next to her ear and then just held her as she needed to be held. She closed her eyes, trying to regain a sense of security in the sanctuary of his arms.

After a few moments, she forced herself to pull slightly away to look into his eyes. Instinctively, she reached up to kiss his cheek. At the same moment, he turned his head as though to release her and their mouths collided.

His entire body stiffened, his shock obvious. But his lips caught and kept hers. Soft and gentle, he gave her the lightest of kisses, as though she were fragile and could shatter at any moment. Warmth and tenderness swelled in her chest and her sense of balance wobbled, her legs feeling like glowing masses of air.

Somewhere far away a commotion sounded, loud voices followed by the door to the storeroom being flung open.

Willa almost protested when Hart's lips pulled away, leaving her dazed and swaying on her feet.

"You sodding bastard." Cam stood on the threshold with his legs braced apart, hands fisted at his sides, the look of astonishment on his face mutating into a feral snarl when he took in their embrace and her ravaged gown. "I'll kill you for this."

Chapter Seven

Hart barely registered Cam's words on account of the pounding in his ears. Realizing he still held Willa's soft sumptuousness in his arms, he gently disengaged from her, guiding her to sink into one of the hard chairs at the small wooden table.

Turning to face his friend, he said, "I can explain."

"Stubble it, you white livered son of a bitch." Cam's voice shook with fury. "You will explain it to my saber while I'm running you through."

Willa's murmur of protest distracted Cam. He moved to kneel before her, wrapping his hands over hers. "Willa? Did he harm you?"

She held the fabric of her torn gown together over her chest to cover herself. "No, of course not."

"He tore your gown." Disbelief filled Cam's voice as he surged to his feet and spun to face Hart, a savage gleam in his eyes. "You bastard."

Still trying to gain his bearings, Hart planted his feet, readying himself for Cam's assault. "It is not what it seems."

"No? I find you alone in a room with the door closed." He stalked toward Hart. "Your hands were all over her."

"Cam, don't be absurd." Willa pushed a tendril from her face, cheeks rosy against porcelain skin. Her mass of chestnut curls had partly fallen down, tumbling about her shoulders. Hart forced his eyes away from the extra bit of pale flesh left exposed by the torn décolletage of her gown.

"Hartwell didn't attack me," she said, the words weary. "He saved me from a man who attacked me in the alley. If it hadn't been for His Grace, who knows what would have happened."

"Saved you?" Cam tilted a look at her. "What were you doing alone in the alley?"

"I was riding with Augustus." She glanced at Hart and then back to her cousin. "I decided to alight and walk the rest of the way."

"Alone? Willa, what were you thinking?" Cam's voice rose in exasperation. "This is London, not some country village."

"The traffic was intolerable," she said. "So you see, we owe Hartwell our thanks."

Hart barely registered the exchange. All he heard was that she'd been with Bellingham.

"Allow me to understand," Cam said to Hart. "My cousin was attacked and you saved her from certain ravishment only to tip the velvet yourself?"

Willa blanched at the coarse language. "Cam!"

His eyes blazed. "Do you deny it, Hartwell?"

Hart's gut tightened. How could he refute it? Their

tongues might not have been involved, but there was no denying that kiss. As fleeting as it had been, one could barely qualify the brief meeting of lips as a kiss, yet a part of him instinctively comprehended the course of his life had just been altered.

Just as suddenly, the sting of remorse gutted him. She'd been vulnerable and frightened and he had taken unconscionable liberties. "You are right, of course," he said to Cam. "Mine were the actions of a blackguard."

He barely had time to register the sight of Cam's fist coming at him before it connected with his jaw. Pain exploded in his cheekbone and he staggered backwards under the force of the blow. Not that he would have defended himself. He deserved to be thrashed. Steadying himself, Hart fingered his throbbing jaw. "I will make it right."

Grimacing, Cam cradled his fist. "Damn right you will."

"Without a doubt." Pain screamed in his jaw. "I shall seek a special license."

"What?" Willa rocketed to her feet. "Stop being so honorable, Hartwell. Tell him the truth." She wheeled around to Cam. "I forced him. I threw myself in his arms and practically begged him not to let me go. He was too gentlemanly to refuse me."

"Gentlemanly?" Cam shot her a look of furious astonishment. "I cannot believe you would defend him."

"I am doing no such thing." She turned to Hart. "You must tell him the truth."

But he could not, of course. To admit that she'd encouraged him in any way would impugn her reputation even further. She'd been shaken and frightened. He shouldn't have touched her. He had behaved reprehensibly and would willingly pay the price. "The truth is my actions were dishonorable even if my intentions were not. I shall make it right by marrying you."

She froze, clearly stunned. Then suspicion gleamed in those mahogany eyes. "Is that the true reason for this sudden attack of gallantry?"

His heart twinged. She doubted his intentions? Not that he blamed her after what he had just allowed to happen.

Willa's hands fisted on her hips. "I am not marrying anyone."

Ignoring her, Cam addressed Hart in concrete tones. "You shall marry immediately." It was a statement, not a question.

"Without question. It would be my honor." Then, quietly and more urgently, "I assure you, it was not my intent to dishonor Lady Wilhelmina in any way."

"Mind your words, Hartwell." Cam's body trembled with fury. "I'm still debating whether to let you marry into the family or just kill you and have done with it."

"Are you mad?" Willa burst out. "I was attacked by a footpad and he rescued me." She gave Hartwell a beseeching look. "Tell him."

Hart's gaze slipped to the fullness of her mouth, remembering its glorious taste. "There is no denying what Camryn saw here with his own eyes."

She reddened all the way to her ears. "You are both reacting precipitously." Gulping a breath, she turned to Cam. "No one has to know. We will just go on as before."

Weary lines marked Cam's face. "Lady Rawdon knows something of what happened here. She saw Hartwell carrying you and was more than pleased to alert me to your situation." He sighed. "Your reputation cannot survive another scandal."

"We shall marry," Hart said in decisive tones, certain of the inherent rightness of his decision. "It is the only answer."

Willa's arms crossed under her chest, drawing his eye to her abundant, softly quivering bosom. One that would soon be his to cherish—along with the rest of this heavenly woman. The thought of it triggered a surprising burst of gladness in him.

But she didn't seem to be reacting with the same equanimity. "You two and your misplaced sense of honor are not going to force me into marriage with a man who has made his disdain for me quite clear."

A glancing pain stung Hart's chest. "Do you find the idea of marriage to me so abhorrent?"

"I won't consent," she said stubbornly to Cam. "My reputation be gone. I won't be forced into a silly charade of a marriage for no good reason. I won't do it."

"I cannot force you." Sadness weighted Cam's voice. Willa exhaled with obvious relief, but then Cam turned to Hart. "She leaves me no alternative. I demand satisfaction."

"What! Are you cracked?" Willa blurted. "Don't be a fool. There is not going to be any duel!"

Tension snaked into every muscle in Hart's body. "Name your seconds, Camryn."

Willa whipped around to Hart. "Don't be so beetle brained," she cried. "Cam's a perfect shot. He'll kill you."

"So be it." A sense of calm infused him. "Your honor has to be avenged."

"Avenged?" Willa's voice rose in panic. "What of your mother? You would leave her alone in this world? She has already lost one son. You would condemn her to a life without either of her children?"

"It is not ideal, but I have little choice in the matter." Heaviness settled in his heart. His mother's grief would be unimaginable. "Name your seconds, Camryn."

"Not ideal? Aren't you the last of your line?" she asked in a voice gone shrill with a rising sense of panic.

He nodded in assent without taking his eyes off Cam's stony expression. "What will it be, old friend, bullet or blade?"

"Wait!" Desperation edged her voice. "You must give me time to consider this. If marrying Hartwell is the only alternative to you two killing each other, I should at least have a few days to consider it."

"No." Cam's impenetrable stare moved from Hart to Willa. "I will have your consent now."

"Very well." She threw up her hands. "If you agree not to announce any betrothal until after the house party."

"What house party?" Hart ventured to ask.

"The one I was supposed to invite you to today," Cam said with baleful contempt. "To celebrate Adela's engagement."

"So you agree to withhold any announcement until after the party?" Willa pressed.

"Why?" Suspicion glinted Cam's eyes. "To give you time to find a way to escape the parson's trap? I know you too well, cousin, to fall for that."

"I need time to adjust myself to the idea. Surely that is not too much to ask."

"Very well," Cam relented. "You have a fortnight. But I must make the announcement before the gossips explode this situation into something intolerable."

Hart rubbed his tender jaw. "I'll speak with Lady Rawdon and impress upon her how grateful I will be if she holds her tongue."

"I'll see to it that she is invited to the house party," Cam said. "If she is ensconced in the country with us, she can hardly be spreading rumors here in town."

"What if she writes letters to her friends in town while she is at Camryn Hall?" Willa asked.

"Missives can easily be lost if she sends them from the hall," Cam said. "Leave that to me."

The energy and fire seemed to cascade out of Willa, leaving her looking utterly worn out as she sank back into the chair. "Now will one of you go into the alley and retrieve the package I dropped there? I have dire need of it."

"Beg pardon?" Cam looked at her as though she'd lost her mind.

Hart turned for the door. As her husband, he suspected he would often do her bidding, and quite happily. He might as well begin now. Buoyed by the thought, he suppressed a smile. "I shall retrieve it."

. . .

"What happened to your face?"

Hart fingered his split lip. "It is nothing."

Willa sat opposite the duke as his post chaise carried them away from London a week after her attack. "Did Cam do that when he hit you?"

"No, this is a bit more recent, an accident last evening. Nothing of importance."

Willa exchanged glances with Addie, who sat beside her.

Hart and Cam were across from them, their backs to the coachman.

Cam stretched his legs in front of him, looking deceptively relaxed. Sitting with his back straight, Hart affected a more formal posture. The older ladies, including her mother, rode ahead in Cam's conveyance.

"Were you involved in some sort of fisticuffs?" she pressed.

"I tripped."

Into somebody's fist, no doubt. She didn't believe him for a moment, yet she allowed him to dismiss the matter. She had far more pressing problems with which to concern herself. The steady beat of the moving carriage lulled them into a strained silence for a time, the horses' thudding hooves and the clacking of the moving wheels filling the air. Staring blindly out the window, her stomach ached with nervous tension. She had so little time to find a way out of this sham of a betrothal. But find it she would.

She caught the duke sneaking a furtive glance at her every now and again. He looked darkly handsome today. Instead of his usual all-black ensemble, Hartwell wore a deep blue waistcoat embellished with tiny, intricate designs. A solid jacket of the same shade brought out the color of his slate eyes. The strong contours of his thighs were encased in form-fitting brown breeches. Willa pulled back as far as possible in her seat, so that her knees would not bump those long, masculine legs.

Adela's gaze flitted from Hart to Willa and back again. Willa could see her sister's mind working. She had confided the truth to Addie, who'd been both shocked by and impressed with Willa's involvement in the tea shop.

Addie fidgeted in her seat. One of her sparkling blue eyes narrowed. Willa knew that look. It meant Addie was in serious contemplation and would soon share her revelations. She closed her eyes and murmured a prayer that her sister would keep her thoughts to herself. Just this once.

"Becoming a duchess would be no hardship," Addie finally said, breaking the silence.

Hart's dark brows drew together in amused surprise. Her ears burning, Willa elbowed her sister in the ribs. "Don't be a goose. There's more to it than that."

Addie shifted out of reach of Willa's elbow. "It's not as though he's an ugly old troll. Far from it."

"Thank you, Lady Adela." Hartwell dipped his chin.

She smiled brightly. "You are most welcome."

"I should be pleased to call you sister," he continued.

Willa glared at her. If only she were close enough to pinch her sister without detection. Instead, she had to settle for inflecting a warning tone into her voice. "Addie."

Hart's dark gaze focused on her. "Perhaps you'd care to explain your concerns so I might ease them."

"Why did you thrash Augustus at university?"

His assertive lips pressed together. "How is that relevant to our betrothal?"

"I should like to know what brings you to violence." She gestured toward his red, swollen lip. "You seem to have a tendency toward fisticuffs."

Addie leaned forward with interest. "You pummeled Augustus?" She slapped her knee and laughed. "I should have liked to see that."

"Pity it isn't Addie you're courting," Cam said wryly. "Your work here would be complete."

"How am I to know whether you hide a brutal nature?" Willa asked. "You refuse to explain the injury to your lip."

"Very well." Hart ran a light finger over his mouth. "This occurred last evening. I was waylaid by footpads after departing Brooks."

Willa inhaled. "You were attacked?"

"You should have taken the carriage," Cam said. "Dukes cannot expect to safely walk unescorted in the evening."

"Obviously I am not yet accustomed my new exalted status."

"What happened?" Addie's words were full of excited anticipation. "How did you elude them?"

"I persuaded them to reconsider their actions."

Willa tilted her head. "With your fists, no doubt."

"I won't apologize for defending myself when provoked." Hart's certain tone held no trace of contrition. "However, I've never raised my hand to a woman and never would. As your husband, I will protect and honor you as no other."

Her protector. A warm lush feeling welled up inside of Willa, but she refused to allow herself to be a pawn in his battle with Augustus. "That does not answer my question about the thrashing you gave the earl."

His face closed off. "I cannot discuss the incident at Cambridge."

Disappointment filled her chest. Had he pummeled the earl out of jealousy? It was entirely possible his sole interest in her lay in keeping her out of his nemesis' hands. "Cannot or will not?"

"It is a matter of honor." His expression was inscrutable. "I cannot say anymore."

Willa looked to Cam for help, but he shrugged. "He

never would say. I was away that week. I'd gone home because Father was ill." He gave her a meaningful look. "But Hart has long maintained the altercation involved a matter of honor and I take him at his word."

Frustrated, she tried again. "At least tell me the source of your enmity with him."

Hart's already sharp features hardened, giving him an even more intimidating presence than usual. "It is one and the same. I cannot." His eyes narrowed on her. "Why is something so long past of such concern to you?"

"Is it past? Or am I a pawn in your game with him?"

A vein pulsed in Hart's forehead. "If you think what occurred between us after your attack had anything to do with Gus Manning, you couldn't be more mistaken."

Willa inhaled sharply at his indelicate reference to their kiss. Cam stiffened, except for his hand, which curled into a fist so tight his knuckles whitened.

"And it was awfully kind of His Grace to retrieve your lost tea," Addie added.

"What lost tea?" Cam looked from Addie to Willa. This time she did pinch Addie. And she added a little twist to it to make sure her sister received the message.

"Ouch!" Addie jerked away and rubbed her arm, shooting Willa a look of wounded outrage.

Cam's gaze narrowed. "Why were you taking your tea to the coffee house?"

"You might as well tell him. There is no shame in it." Addie inched further out of Willa's reach. "After all, you're selling your tea for a noble cause."

"Selling your tea?" Cam's voice throbbed with outraged disbelief. "Tell me Addie is mistaken." Wincing, Willa pressed her lips together. Cam exhaled slowly through his nostrils. "Now you've taken to engaging in trade?"

"It's not like that—" Addie began.

"You have said quite enough, thank you." Willa cut her off. Straightening, she met Cam's angry gaze. "I donate my tea to the coffee house. It is sold to provide a way for the women who work there to provide for themselves and their children. I do not profit from it."

Cam's mouth fell open as a tide of color swept his face. "This is beyond belief. You *are* engaged in trade. Why are you so determined to ruin yourself?"

Hartwell cleared his throat and shifted in his seat. "It is for a laudable cause."

Cam glared at Hart. "You knew about this?"

"I only suspected."

Willa turned her attention to Hart. "Is my involvement the reason you are trying to close the coffee house?"

"He is?" Addie looked at Hart. "Are you?"

Hart's lips pushed inward. "My interest in the building is purely related to business. It is an ideal location for my London headquarters."

"You will be condemning the women who work there to a life on the street," Willa said heatedly.

Hart frowned. "Why can the enterprise not be relocated?"

"It is costly to do so and would make it more difficult for the workers to find their way to the coffee house if it is removed too far away."

"Willa." Cam interrupted, his frustration plain. "What else don't I know about your clandestine activities? Have you decided to start treading the boards as well?"

"Willa on the stage?" Addie giggled. "I should like to see that."

"I am well past worrying about being ruined," Willa said. "Why shouldn't I engage in an activity that assists the less fortunate?"

Sighing, Cam closed his eyes and pinched the bridge of his nose. "Having never had sisters, I clearly know nothing about managing females." He looked to Hart. "I cannot wait until she is your concern."

"Neither can I." A slow smile of genuine delight opened across the duke's face, his midnight blue eyes glowed as they held her gaze. "I don't suppose Lady Wilhelmina can be managed, but I shall certainly take pleasure in the trying of it."

Chapter Eight

Restless and frustrated with Willa's continued reluctance, Hartwell slipped out for a brisk ride shortly after their arrival at Camryn Park. He galloped over wide expanses of open parkland, releasing tension as he breathed in the fresh country air and enjoyed the cacophony of sounds from swooshing trees and chattering birds. Spotting a glimmer from a pond hidden in a secluded copse of trees, he dismounted and led the animal toward the lush greenery surrounding the pond.

Just before he came out of the clearing, the sounds of splashing water halted him. Someone was taking a swim. He looked toward the noise and his mouth went dry.

A womanly form, clad only in a shift, emerged from beneath the surface, water streaming from her curves. *Willa*. She dipped back to wet her hair. Her full, upright breasts arched up, straining against the wet, diaphanous shift that left little to the imagination. Desire and want slammed through him. Staggering backward, his hand shot up to seize an overhead branch to steady himself.

He hadn't realized how lush her breasts were. They were full and heavy under the now transparent chemise that outlined their every curve. He could see the rosy pink outline of her areolas and the hardened nubs at the center of them.

She turned away and dove back under the surface. He lost his breath when her shift floated up in the water as she did so, exposing an exquisitely rounded, white bottom which curved above the water for a tantalizing moment before disappearing under the surface. Re-emerging, she flipped over to float on her back and he almost lost his mind. Her lavish breasts jutted skyward as if in exquisite offering to the sun gods, the cold water swelling their rosy tips to pert splendor beneath the gossamer cloth. His gaze trailed downward to the shadow between her legs.

Heat pooled in his groin. It was as if he were seeing the genuine Willa for the first time. She moved with pure abandon, seizing the pleasure of the sun and water for herself, meshing with the natural surroundings. It was not only the sight of her body, smooth and rounded to feminine perfection, but also the way she moved through the water with simple, unrestrained pleasure, that shook him. That cool aloofness she usually showed the world fell away. Stripped of all artifice, Willa was spellbinding. The pure intimacy of the moment made his throat ache. Any lingering doubts about making her his wife melted away.

She floated along, eyes closed, with an occasional lazy swirl of her arms. Her languorous gaze turned in his direction and they locked eyes. His heart sped up as silence stretched between them, as if she didn't comprehend his presence in the midst of her private, sun-dazed revelry. Then her eyes widened.

"Hartwell?" She startled into action—jerky, panicked movements of flailing arms and shapely legs splashing in the water. And an abundance of other wiggling feminine parts that made his mouth go dry. She finally sank, leaving only her head bobbing above the water's surface.

He belatedly remembered himself. Much too late, of course. In a strangled voice, he uttered, "I do beg your pardon," and pivoted, giving her his back.

"I most certainly will not beg your pardon!" Her outraged voice trembled with agitation amidst more splashing noises. "How long have you been standing there ogling me?"

"I had no intention of—" His tongue tangled. He *had* been leering at her like the worst kind of lecher. He hadn't meant to watch her. He certainly shouldn't have. But really, what red-blooded male could have looked away from Willa's lush, womanly form floating in the water as if she were Aphrodite herself? He half expected flowers to spring up under her feet once she stepped back onto dry land. "I took my mount for a run and spotted the water. My intention was to give my animal his fill."

"It appears you looked your fill instead."

The sound of rushing of water behind him suggested she'd pulled herself out of the pond. His mind didn't have to work terribly hard to imagine what she looked like with the water-drenched translucent fabric of her shift plastered against the hard pearl tips of her breasts.

"It was the behavior of a scoundrel and a blackguard." His back still to her, he focused on his mount grazing nearby.

"I shall leave you to your privacy."

"A little late for that, don't you think?" she muttered.

"Whatever I can do to make it up to you, I shall do." As if that were possible. They both knew he couldn't unsee the vision of her damp, nubile body glistening in the sun.

Clothes rustled behind him. "Actually, there is a way you can make amends."

"There is?" The calculation he heard in her voice made his skin prickle.

"I've wanted to meet with you alone."

"Dare I be hopeful?"

"Do not be disgusting," she said sharply. "You may turn around now."

He obliged, steeling himself to meet her accusing gaze. Only he turned to find she wasn't looking at him. Instead, she'd turned away to wring water from the white cloth in her hands. Which allowed him to sneak another look at her. Good lord, she was a goddess. Her cascade of chestnut hair fell in ringlets about her shoulders. Water rivulets dampened her dress, which clung to her sweetly curved bottom as she squeezed liquid from her shift. He swallowed hard. Her shift. Which meant that under that gown, she wore…nothing.

He felt lightheaded. Surely the god of temptation was punishing him for some grievous sin from his past. "What did you wish to discuss?"

"How to put an end to this ludicrous betrothal."

The words hit him like a blow to the gut. "So Cam was correct in assuming you had cause to delay the announcement of our happy news."

"You saved me from a footpad," she said in a determined voice. "You shouldn't be punished for your chivalry by being chained to me into perpetuity."

"Perhaps I care to be chained." His deepened his voice. "Especially after today." Her cheeks warmed. He'd wager her ears were red, too, but that glistening curtain of curls hid them from view.

"Besides," he continued, "I'm easily bored and, if the past few days are any indication, life with you is bound to be most interesting. What with footpads, clandestine tea enterprises, and a marriage proposal, I've barely had time to follow recent developments."

"A marriage proposal?" She uttered a sound of derision. "I don't recall being asked for my hand in marriage. You and Cam arranged it."

"You acquiesced."

"Under the strain of dire consequences. You threatened to kill my cousin. It was most romantic. Every girl's dream."

"To be fair, Cam is the one who challenged me, but if that is all—" He promptly fell onto one knee, taking her soft hand, with its long slim fingers, into his own. "Lady Wilhelmina, I admire you above all others. Will you make me the happiest of men by agreeing to become my wife?"

She snatched her hand away. "No, that is not all and I most certainly will not. Do be serious. We are barely acquainted."

"After today, I would say that isn't exactly true." He pushed to his feet, raking his eyes over her abundant curves. "I look forward with great anticipation to coming to know you much more intimately."

Heat suffused her face. She parted her lips and brought her hand to her neck, her chest moving more quickly. The air between them swirled with carnal awareness.

"You made your true feelings quite clear at my mother's dinner party in town," she finally said, her voice shaky.

Cold remorse filled his lungs. Of course she'd want nothing to do with someone who behaved as caddishly as he had after he'd stolen that kiss. "My behavior was that of the worst blackguard. I deeply regret my actions of that evening."

"It is in the past," she said carefully. "What is best is for us both to move forward. In order to do that, you must release me from this betrothal."

"I will do no such thing."

"Why must you be so obstinate?"

"It would be dishonorable not to proceed as planned. And I think perhaps you need me to keep you out of harm's way."

Her large mocha eyes held his. "I gather we are speaking of Augustus now."

Bellingham. The realization she couldn't get that whoreson out of her mind clogged the air in his lungs. "So that's the way of it."

She frowned. "What's the way of it?"

The lady had no idea what depravity Bellingham was capable of. And honor, in the form of a long-ago promise, prohibited him from enlightening her. But he could keep her safe. Determination hardened in him. "There is nothing to left to discuss." His words were curt and harder than frozen tundra. "We will marry. It is done."

• • •

Exasperated, Willa dropped to the ground to pull on her

ankle boots. He'd intruded on her private oasis, piercing the tranquility that always came over her whenever she went for a swim at the pond. She squinted up at him, shielding her eyes against the sun with her hand. The sun shone behind him, casting a bright halo around his darkened silhouette. It outlined his tall, hard body, defining the curve of muscle in his thighs. The sunlight streaming through his white shirt allowed her to take in the turn of strength in his arms. Her pulse flowed faster at his nearness.

She struggled to collect her thoughts. Perhaps the truth of what happened at the inn would cure him of his obstinate resolve to marry her. One he understood she was already as good as ruined, surely he'd relinquish his gentlemanly insistence, and this absurd competition with Augustus. "If you insist on pursuing this course of action, we must speak truthfully about the earl."

His eyes darkened. "Bellingham?"

Anxiety stretched in her chest. She'd never spoken of this to anyone. "You understand I have a history with his lordship."

His expression remained inscrutable. "Go on."

"I did want to marry him once, very much so."

"Then I can only request that you refrain from any indiscretions, at least until you've given me an heir and a couple of spares." The words were sharp and cold, all traces of his previous warmth gone. "Just so there can be no doubt about lineage and succession."

Her mouth fell open. "Indiscretions?" Nausea bubbled in her chest. "Is this your way of informing me you plan to take mistresses?" She knew many *ton* marriages were marked by open affairs on both sides, but she could never countenance that kind of union for herself.

He examined her face. "Would you care if I did?"

Her body sank inward to absorb the blow of his words, as if he'd physically struck her. The duke planned to humiliate her with his affairs—just as her father had her mother. Tears prickled her nose. Like all men, he could not be trusted.

"Clearly, we hold differing views on the matrimonial state," she bit out, proud she managed to inject a coolness she didn't feel into the words. "It is fortunate we've realized our mistake before proceeding any further." Shoulders back, chin tilted upward, she moved to walk past him.

"I have no intention of taking a mistress." His large body stepped in her path. "There is only one woman I want and she stands before me." The profound tenderness in his expression stole her breath. "You are all the woman I need."

He lowered his face and gentle lips covered hers, his masculine scent filling her nose. He cradled her cheeks in his large hands and tilted his head to better take possession of her mouth. His lips were both firm and lush, imbuing the intimacy with intense emotion. Heat flooded her insides. The tip of his tongue touched her lower lip, asking for entry. She opened her mouth immediately and wrapped her hands around his neck.

Their tongues met, flickered together, and then mated in full stroking motions. Shivering with pleasure, she tasted the lingering essence of tea and cheroot, and an explosion of other nuances in the velvet warmth of his mouth. Hart's tongue probed and demanded, tasted and devoured. His large hands closed over the swell of her bottom, cupping and massaging the sensitive mounds, urging her closer.

She went willingly. Shocking herself, she clawed at Hart's

shirt, desperate to feel the warm, bare skin underneath. When at last she reached the smooth, hard musculature of his back, his skin burned under her fingers. Her body throbbing with need, she pushed her heavy breasts against his chest, the curve of her body clinging to the determined lines of his. His arousal pressed into her softness. Just when it seemed as if nothing could stop her wantonness, an indignant voice rang out.

"Unhand her this instant."

The shrill tone in Augustus' outraged words pierced Willa's abandon. Instead of floating on a cloud of warm pleasure, she returned to earth, to the feel of the hard ground beneath her boots and the press of the afternoon sun on her back. She broke away from Hart as though touched by fire, her cheeks and ears burning. The earl sat atop his gelding, watching them with a blanched face contorted with rage. Dismounting, he strode toward them, his body tensed with challenge.

Hart turned to Augustus with arrogant confidence, satisfaction etched in every line of his face. "I beg your pardon?" His cavalier tone suggested no trace of shame or humiliation at being caught in flagrante. Quite the contrary. Instead, he exuded the air of a man greatly enjoying himself.

Anxiety shot through her. She could not bear for this tawdry scene to become fodder for gossip among the house guests. It would humiliate her mother and taint the festivities planned in honor of Addie's engagement.

Hart seemed amused by Augustus' obvious distress and appeared to be in no hurry to alleviate it for him. "You have no right to interfere here. This is none of your concern."

Augustus' eyes widened. "None of my concern?" He

dismounted in a quick motion and took a step toward them. "You, sir, have corrupted this lady and I shall call you out for damaging her honor."

Another duel. Over her. Willa's head spun, and not just from Hart's kiss.

"You needn't concern yourself with my affianced bride's virtue." Taking Willa's arm, he tucked it into his elbow, signaling he had rights to her that no other man had.

The earl's imperious features froze. "Your bride?" he said with a harsh laugh. "The Lady Wilhelmina? I think not."

"What you think is of no consequence to me or my betrothed."

Augustus' gaze shifted to Willa's face. "I have heard nothing of a betrothal. If you think to spare yourself from the dueling field by hiding behind her skirts—"

Hart took a step toward Augustus, his tone full of lethal warning. "As I said, our betrothal is none of your concern. You have no rights to the lady."

"Ah, but she and I have unfinished business." The earl ran in his eyes over Willa's body, his eyes lingering on her breasts. She flushed, crossing her arms protectively over her chest. "Do you truly believe you are the only man to have sampled her abundant charms?"

Willa stiffened. Shame and dread shot up her spine at the mention of her ruination. Clearly, the earl meant to destroy her once and for all.

"You will speak no words against the lady nor do harm to her reputation." The cut lines of Hart's face sharpened into a menacing mask, his still-untucked shirt adding to an aura of untamed ferociousness. "Or I warn you I shall not bother to wait for the dueling field. I will beat you to a bloody pulp. I promise you another thrashing that will make Cambridge seem like a glove to the face in comparison."

Warmth spilled into her belly, radiating out to her limbs at the fierceness of Hart's tone. No one had ever defended her honor this way. Not even her family. Although they'd sought to shield her by ignoring the swirling rumors of her ruin, no one had ever stood up for her as Hart did now.

Augustus stared, for the first time betraying the faintest sign of alarm. "When is this supposed betrothal going to take place?"

Willa lifted her chin and sealed her fate. "It is already set. His Grace has spoken to Camryn." Her hand remained in the comforting strength of the crook of her betrothed's elbow. Her *betrothed*. She'd never intended to become anyone's betrothed. But, to her immense surprise, the sound of that appealed to her.

"Is that so?" the earl said coldly. "And why is it no one seems aware of this most joyous news?"

"We are waiting until after the house party to make the announcement." Willa placed her other hand on Hart's elbow, so that she almost cradled his arm. "So as not to interfere with Adela and Race's betrothal celebrations."

"You needn't concern yourself any further." Warning saturated Hart's words. "She is under my protection now and forever more. An insult against my lady is a slight against me and will be dealt with accordingly. Now, I suggest that you mount your beast and leave us to our privacy."

It was not a request. Augustus' eyes moved over Willa, lingering longer than was appropriate. Hart cursed under his breath and stepped forward, but Willa tightened her hold on his arm, silently imploring him to desist.

"I will withdraw. For now." The earl swung up onto his horse. "But I warn you, this is far from over." With that, he urged his horse onward at a leisurely pace, not appearing the least bit rushed or intimidated.

When he'd moved a distance away, Willa turned toward Hart and took a deep breath, steeling herself for the questions he would inevitably ask. Of course he would want to clarify Augustus' pointed implications. If they were to marry, she knew the time had come to answer Hart's questions honestly.

He regarded her with clouded deep blue eyes, but his tone was easy. "That settles it then."

"Settles it?" She pressed a hand flat against the heavy disappointment in her stomach. He was leaving her. Just an hour ago, she might have welcomed it. But no longer.

"Yes." He walked over to his mount and picked up the reins. "No bits of muslin for me and no strange men in your bed." He walked back over and offered her his arm. "If that kiss is any indication, I'll have no need to look further than the marriage bed to satisfy my needs."

• • •

With a loud cry of outrage, Augustus hurled the brandy decanter. It shattered against the stone hearth, spewing shards of glass onto the faded Aubusson carpet. Standing in the dark-paneled study at Bellingham Park, he battled to calm the storm in his head.

Up until now, he'd been fairly certain he had been the only man to kiss Willa, to know her intimately. Now Hartwell had infringed on what was his.

Augustus' plan to keep Willa untouched by another man until he was ready for her had worked beautifully up until this moment. It had almost been too easy. For years she had dangled like succulent low-hanging fruit before the entire *ton,* but no idiot dared step forward to pluck her. Until today. And it had to be Hartwell, now a duke, no less. Not someone who could be intimidated or bought off. Though perhaps blackmail remained a possibility. He would have his man of affairs look into it.

He closed his eyes, trying to block out the loathsome images of Willa in Hartwell's arms, her supple body arched up against his. She'd behaved like a common whore who'd spread her legs for any man. Unlike how she had been with him. Her nervous, stilted kisses at the inn had been anything but welcoming. She'd even put up a struggle, unaware she fought the inevitable.

The thought of her with Hartwell made his head pound. Dark jealousy gouging his chest, he slammed his fist onto his desk and swept everything off its surface. The books and artifacts fell with a thud on the rug. His fit of fury was punctuated by a polite rap on the door and the butler entered to announce that the earl's solicitor awaited his pleasure.

Once he was shown in, James Ogden, a short, sturdy man in spectacles, went straight to the purpose for his visit. "My lord, you lost 10,000 guineas in a single bet last week."

"Yes." He examined his fingernails. "What of it?"

"My lord, I must warn you the excessive betting is doing severe damage to your financial situation."

"Why are you bothering me about a silly wager?" Augustus said impatiently. "I have made bigger ones."

"Yes, indeed," the solicitor said. "That is part of the

problem."

"How dare you presume to tell me how to manage my affairs? Perhaps you should remember your place."

Ogden coughed. "My place is to handle your financial affairs. I thought you should be aware that it might be difficult to meet certain expenses in the coming months."

Augustus adopted a condescending tone, one he'd use with a child. "Then take out more markers. Just see that you take care of things."

"Incurring more debt would not be a wise course to take. Perhaps you should consider cutting expenses—"

Augustus had heard enough. He rose to signal the end of the conversation. "Perhaps you should find a position elsewhere. I've no further use for your services. Get out of my sight."

Ignoring the man's departure, his thoughts bounced back to the sight of Willa in Hartwell's arms. He couldn't wait to teach her a lesson, to punish her for letting another man touch her. And given Ogden's concerns about finances, her dowry would come in quite handy as well.

The butler reappeared with a packet. "My lord, this came for you today. From a man who identified himself as a Bow Street runner."

"Excellent. Just what I've been waiting for." Eager anticipation supplanted the earl's irritation. He could only hope these papers contained the information he sought. Tearing the package open, he scanned the documents, finally finding just what he needed to make Willa his. He smiled. It wouldn't be long now before he brought the haughty princess to her knees. The delicious sense of long-awaited satisfaction swelled his member.

He refocused his attention on the butler. "Benton, what is the name of the new maid? The pretty one with the brown hair and big brown eyes."

Benton stiffened. "Mary, my lord?"

"Mary, yes. Send her in to clean up this mess."

"My lord, William, the footman, can see to it. It is his duty."

Augustus waved an impatient hand. His breeches were fast becoming uncomfortably tight. "I determine who does what around here. Send Mary in now."

A few minutes later, after a tentative knock on the study door, Mary entered with her head bowed, a riot of brown curls escaping the sides of her demure cap. She knelt to pick up the mess on the floor. Augustus watched her for a moment from behind his desk. He tried to remember her story. Ah, yes, she came from the village. The father was dead and the girl's earnings supported the mother and younger siblings. He walked around to the front of his desk and leaned his hip against it as the maid went about her task. She was a petite little thing, a mere girl really, with not much meat on her bones. Not that it mattered. He began to unfasten his breeches.

"Come here, Mary. There is something else I need you to take care of for me."

Chapter Nine

"You have terrible aim," Addie said gaily to Race after he missed all but one pin in his first throw at Skittles.

The guests had scattered across the lawn behind the manor house. Some played croquet while others tried their hand at battlecock and shuttledore. The older guests, ensconced in comfortable chairs grouped together on the grass, sipped lemonade and watched the goings-on.

Race's brows waggled in his rough-hewn face. "My aim is perfect when it counts—as you shall soon see." Addie colored, but an agitated Augustus interrupted the couple's flirtation.

"Enough nonsense. It is devil warm out here. Pray do finish your turn so we can adjourn for some lemonade."

Race advanced on the pins for his tipping shot. The guests playing at Skittles had broken into foursomes. The sisters were paired off with Race and the earl, which Willa suspected Augustus had orchestrated. So far, the earl behaved as though yesterday's encounter had never occurred, as if he hadn't caught her acting the wanton with Hartwell. He'd vanished afterward, likely retiring to his neighboring estate before returning this morning to rejoin the guests. There was a certain smugness in his demeanor that unsettled her. He wasn't behaving like a man who'd lost his long-standing battle with the duke.

Looking off across the wide expanse of lawn to where some men were engaged in target practice, Willa could make out Hartwell's towering form next to Cam's lean, sinewy one. Bringing her fingertips to her lips, she recalled the startling pleasure of Hart's uncompromising mouth rubbing against hers, demanding a response. It had been starkly different from the gentle, almost deferential, way he'd kissed her after the attack at the coffee house. He was a man of contrasts and she couldn't deny how much every side of him intrigued her.

"Willa, it is your turn," called Addie. "Do stop your woolgathering."

"Oh, of course." Shaking Hart from her mind, Willa stepped forward and threw her ball at the Skittles, pouring her nervous anticipation into it. She knocked six down and moved forward for her tipping shot. Throwing from just beside the pins, she made the final throw with precise determination and succeeded in laying them all out.

Addie clapped her hands. "That was very well done."

Race whistled low with appreciation. "You always did have a mean throw, Willa."

"Not particularly ladylike, but it certainly did the job," said the earl, stepping forward for his turn.

Addie scowled openly at Augustus' rude remark, but

Willa bit back a retort. Her scalp tingled at the way he looked at her, with the confident precision of a bird of prey honing in on his victim.

The earl hurled the ball in one quick, decisive stroke. Sun glistening in his blond curls, he moved with a lanky ease, knocking all of the pins over with one blow. "Behold," he said to his brother gesturing to the downed pins, "how Skittles is correctly played."

Race grinned. "You've quite unmanned me, which is very badly done of you in front of my betrothed." He offered Addie his arm. "Come, my dear, let us leave this braggart to his pins. We shall endeavor to find an activity at which I do excel." Addie blushed and giggled, looking quite happy to be led away on Race's arm.

Left alone with Augustus, and eager to be away from him, Willa said, "Shall we go for lemonade?"

"In a moment." He offered her his arm. "Walk with me for a spell." When she hesitated, he said, "Come now, we are to be family and it is just a stroll about the lawn in full view of the other guests."

Shaking off her lingering unease, she reluctantly took his arm. "Very well."

They started at a leisurely pace about the grass and drew more than a few curious looks from the guests. The elderly Mrs. Beasley didn't bother with subtlety; she pointedly drew up her lorgnette to examine them from her seated position among the older guests.

Willa planted a pleasantly bland smile on her face. Thankfully, a straw bonnet covered her burning ears and the day's warmth might account for any blush upon her cheeks. The thinly veiled interest they drew came as no surprise considering her rumored history with the earl, and the duke's recent attentions to her had not gone unnoticed. "I think you should reconsider my offer," the earl said.

Fidgeting with the pendant of her necklace, Willa asked, "What offer is that?"

"Come now." Condescension drenched his words. "I speak of marriage, as you are well aware."

"That is not possible." She blinked, then smiled with a nod at the curious Mrs. Beasley before continuing in a pleasant tone. "I have an understanding with Hartwell, as you are well aware."

"I suggest you reconsider."

"I cannot."

"Cannot or will not?"

"They are one and the same. I've given my word."

"A woman's word is rarely to be taken seriously." He smiled indulgently. "Come now, Willa, I will make you a fine husband. I regret what occurred at the inn. Allow me make it right. You deserve for people to know you are not a woman of loose morals."

The pull of their shared childhood tugged at Willa's chest. For a fleeting moment, she recognized the boy she'd once cared for, now standing before her offering redemption. Yet the thought of his hands on her… "You must accept my decision."

"It is regrettable that you do not know what is in your best interests." The earl paused to greet a passing guest before continuing. "It would mean your complete and total ruination if people were to learn that you are not only a probable trollop, but also a tradeswoman to boot."

Surprise clogged the air in her lungs. Good lord. He

knew about the coffee shop. "I don't know what you mean."

"Once we're wed, it will all be in the past." He patted her hand where it rested upon his arm. "I shall always protect and guide you."

She lost her footing and he caught her arm before she could stumble, smoothly keeping them both walking at a sedate pace. Anyone watching would no doubt see a gentile pair out for an uneventful stroll. Willa's panicked thoughts coalesced with painful clarity. "You mean to threaten me into marrying you."

Augustus nodded toward Lady Rawdon, who played at battlecock and shuttledore. The lady's appreciative eyes ran over the earl's strong masculine form.

"Threat is such an unpleasant term," he said lightly, ignoring Lady Rawdon's appraisal. "Just think of it as gentle persuasion."

Anxiety filled her chest. "Why would you want a female of questionable virtue as your countess?"

"You came to me that day an innocent." His mouth firmed. "And I choose to overlook any indiscretion you have committed with Hartwell."

"Why would you overlook it? You're an earl." She fought to keep her tone free of the desperation swelling inside her chest. "You could have anyone you choose."

"Precisely, and I choose you." The sun glittered in his steel eyes. "Make no mistake, he will never have you."

"So this is about vanquishing Hartwell, not wedding me."

"Only in part. I won't insult you by dissembling. But remember this, I've wanted you from the first, before you were even out of the schoolroom. We both know he only wants you because I do."

Willa's mind swam. How many ways could she ruin herself? She'd come perilously close several times just in the past few days. Now Augustus sought to blackmail her, taking away any choice she might have in her own future. Fury and indignation kindled in her chest. She refused to be his victim again.

"Do your best, sir." She struggled to keep her benign expression for the benefit of the curious spectators following their every move. "I have no interest in becoming your chattel. I have little to lose. I am already as good as ruined."

They strolled past Mr. Dudley, a gentleman of later years, who paused while taking his turn at croquet to stare at them. Only when his embarrassed wife elbowed him in the ribs did he say, "Hmmm? Oh yes dear, I was just perfecting my aim," before turning his attention back to the game and hitting the ball across the grass.

"You have always been too free with your reputation," the earl said once they passed out of earshot, speaking in a calm voice as though he were discussing idle things. "But do tell, will you be so easy with Lady Florinda's as well?"

Her stomach hollowed. "What do you mean to say?"

"Only that you, at least, have considerable appeal." His smile was smug, as though he knew he'd won. "She is rather plain. I suppose Lady Florinda's dowry is acceptable as the Earl of Bromley's daughter, but I doubt she is so cavalier with her reputation." He tugged on her elbow to continue walking. She stumbled blindly along beside him. "And what of Lady Octavia? Imagine how her father will react when he learns the daughter of a viscount has taken to trade."

She forced her leaden feet to move. "Even you would

not be so cruel."

He continued on as though she had not spoken. "And then there is the Widow Grenfell, Pamela. With her minor fortune and even lesser consequence, she would no longer be welcome in the finest homes."

Willa's chest felt as though several large rocks rested upon it. "You have been spying on me."

"I look after my own and make no mistake, you are mine. You have been since that day at the inn, by rights and by society's dictates."

"Do you know why I did it? The coffee shop, I mean."

"I have some idea. The report prepared by the Bow Street runner is most informative."

He'd set a Bow Street runner on her? "Then you understand I did it to help the less fortunate, not to make a profit," she said. "I kept nothing for myself and neither did any of the others."

"What I understand is that if your involvement in trade is made known, you will all be ruined."

Fighting growing panic, she looked blindly at the guests around her. She was trapped and he knew it. She'd never allow Flor or the others to fall into ruin as she had. "I am already promised," she said weakly.

"The gentler sex cannot make such important decisions. We men must do it for you. Cam has let you run wild." He patted her arm. "But I shall guide you."

He would have complete control over her…and the unlimited right to use her body as he pleased. Images from the inn flashed before her, his lips pressing hard against hers, determined hands pulling up her skirt. Swallowing back a swelling wave of despair, she whispered, "I won't do it. I cannot."

"It might take you a while to accustom yourself to the idea." He smiled with a victor's satisfaction. "Fear not, I shall not impose too much upon you in the marriage bed."

"Willa," her mother called from where the older people sat. "Bring the earl in for some lemonade. You look peaked."

"I regret I must return to Town for a few days. I'll anticipate your answer immediately upon my return," Augustus said in a mild voice before turning to flash his bright smile toward her mother, one that usually left women weak in the knees. "Indeed, lemonade would be quite the thing."

Willa shook her head, desperate to be away from him, to find a way out of his trap. "I am unwell. I shall retire."

He tightened his grip on her elbow. "Nonsense. I should like to take lemonade with my betrothed wife."

A pang of anxiety twisted in her stomach. "You are not my betrothed."

"No, but I will be," he answered, smoothly directing her toward the lemonade.

• • •

Turning away from the sight of Willa traversing the lawn on Bellingham's arm, Hart lifted his weapon and squeezed the trigger. The loud popping sound sliced the air as his shot hit wide left of its intended target. He cursed under his breath.

Next to him, Cam chuckled. "You could use more time on the practice field." He focused his concentration on the target several yards ahead of them and squeezed the trigger, scoring a direct hit at the heart of the target. "That is how it's done, old boy. You must actually try to aim."

"I am out of sorts today."

He eyed the placement of Hart's shot on the target. "I begin to see why you declined to accept my duel challenge."

"It would have been badly done of me to shoot you after our long acquaintance." Hartwell focused on reloading his weapon, waving off the servant who stood ready to do it for him.

"All the same, you would do well to avoid calling anyone out any time in the near future," said Cam. Willa's cousin had recovered his good spirits now that the business of Hart and Willa's betrothal would soon be official. The same could not be said for Hart. His somber mood related directly to Willa of course.

The irony of his situation was not lost on him. He planned to marry Willa to save her honor. But, if one believed the rumors and Bellingham's unsubtle insinuations at the pond, it had been lost long ago. That would explain her lack of suitors. It certainly gave credence to what the men at the club had intimated. He kept hearing their voices in his head. *She belongs to Bellingham. Utterly and completely compromised.*

A part of him longed to demand answers from her. As her betrothed husband, he certainly had the right. If she'd already ruined herself, he wasn't honor bound to marry her.

Her strong reaction to Bellingham's insulting manner at the pond came flooding back. Her pain had been palpable. She'd reacted physically, her body shrinking inward as though she'd been hit. Hart's immediate instinct then — and still now — was to shelter her from that pain, and from any hint of disgrace. He never wanted to see that look on her face again.

He'd come to realize it didn't matter if Willa were no longer innocent. Bellingham was a villain who could have easily manipulated a young girl into a regrettable indiscretion. But she hadn't let it defeat her and he admired her for that. Willa carried herself with pride and self-worth. He thought of the way her eyes sparkled when an idea intrigued her mind, and of the cutting sense of humor she often kept hidden.

His all-encompassing desire for her had come to eclipse everything, even her questionable virtue. His body ached for her almost constantly, with a raw intensity which meant Hart would marry Willa any way he could get her. And he would kill to protect her. But what of the lady? Perhaps part of her still wanted Bellingham, particularly if he'd taken her innocence. The thought of it made Hart's chest burn.

He refocused on his target and gently squeezed the trigger. This time with perfect aim.

"Good shot," said Cam admiringly. "You were dead on point." Unable to summon the enthusiasm to continue, Hart quit. He and Cam left the other gentlemen to the shooting practice and headed back to the house.

"The house party concludes in a few days," Cam said as they walked. "I thought perhaps we should announce your betrothal at the ball."

The ball. Just a few days from now. Hart shot his friend a sidelong glance. "My future duchess appears somewhat reticent."

Cam set his jaw. "She has consented. I'm certain Willa will not betray her word." He looked over at his friend. "She appears to take pleasure in your company these last days. Am I mistaken?"

Hart gritted his teeth. How to explain? "No, you are not. Nonetheless, the situation still needs to be attended to. I shall see to it immediately."

• • •

Willa stood by the window in the drawing room which overlooked the garden. She pretended to listen to Mother chatting with Lady Rawdon, but anxious thoughts crowded her mind. The earl had departed shortly after their walk and would soon return expecting her answer. She'd yet to think of a way to avoid succumbing to his ultimatum. Her friends could not be ruined because of her. She would not allow it.

A hush descended upon the room and Willa realized the duke had entered. He strode with purpose, his strong jaw set. Hart's determined manner made him appear all the more formidable. Her heart flickered at the sight of his dark hair and the sharp cut angles of his face. Especially when she remembered that fiery kiss by the pond. Impeccably turned out as usual, he dressed in a gentleman's simple country clothes, yet his air of easy authority enhanced the crisp white shirt, fawn-colored breeches, and gleaming riding boots. Despite his civilized manner and attire, the duke had a hint of danger about him today. Hart greeted the group with polite words, exchanging enough niceties to be appropriate before turning to Willa and offering his arm.

"Will you join me for a walk in the gardens, Lady Wilhelmina?" It was not really a question. His smooth tone was underscored by a steely determination that made him hard to refuse. Even if she wanted to.

"Of course," she replied in her usual reserved public

manner. She turned to the others. "Will you join us? The flowers are quite beautiful this time of year." They all declined, sensibly concluding the duke would not welcome their company. Many of the guests stole a look at the couple as Hart escorted Willa from the room. Her mother positively beamed.

They walked in silence as they headed to the flower gardens. Willa's heart moved faster. She felt very physically aware of herself…and of him. She shook the thoughts away. She must not allow herself to be drawn to this man. Her course was set. Panic welled at the idea of wedding Augustus. But what else could she do? Her friends would not be ruined because of her. She must steel herself and become accustomed to the notion of being the earl's countess—as intolerable as that sounded.

They reached the garden and turned to stroll down one of its many paths. The sweet smell of the flowers flanking the pathway hung in the air. Many were now in full bloom, providing bursts of color along their path.

Hart finally broke the silence. "Camryn intends to announce our betrothal at the ball."

Willa's stomach rolled with dread. There was no way out. "I'm afraid I must decline your offer."

He stilled beside her. "I see. Do you think Camryn will allow you to remain unwed after what occurred between us?"

"No." She couldn't bear to look into his eyes. "I am to be a bride, just not yours."

"Bellingham?" A sharp intake of breath. "You've accepted his suit after all?"

"I have no choice in the matter."

"Wrong, my dear. You do have a choice and you've made it." Controlled anger tinged his voice. "At least admit to it."

She inhaled and met his intense gaze. "The earl knows about my involvement in the coffee house."

His forehead shot up. "You shared the information with him?"

"Hardly. He set someone to spy upon me." She expelled a shaky breath. "He's threatening to use the information against my friends."

"But not against you?"

"I could withstand his assault on my character, but I cannot allow him to do the same to my friends. Their reputations are unimpeachable."

"Unlike yours." His face darkened. "And that bastard means to use it against you. What has he asked of you?"

"He wishes to marry. He expects my answer upon his return from Town."

"I see." His tone emerged harsher than he intended. "Is that what you intend to do?"

It felt as if a fist was lodged in her throat. "I will not let him destroy my friends."

Dark eyes burned into her face. His warm, clean, masculine smell stole over her. "Perhaps your heart lies with Gus."

"It does not." She struggled to keep the rising panic out of her tone. "I have no choice in the matter."

His sharp features firmed. "Then I won't allow you to cry off."

As if either of them had a choice in the matter. "I have faced the humiliation of a tainted reputation. I cannot subject good women to it."

"No harm will come to them. I will see to it."

"How?"

"I do own of the building in which the coffee house is situated."

Her heart sank. "The sale is complete then?"

"It is. I received the papers this morning."

"I fail to see how purchasing the building can protect the reputations of my friends." The words were cool. "Your acquisition does not seem to serve any purpose other than to deprive hardworking women of their livelihood."

"Since I will no longer accept rent from the coffee house, it ceases to be a profit-making enterprise. As the Duchess of Hartwell, it will be your first charitable endeavor."

"My first charitable endeavor?" Confusion clouded her mind. "You aren't forcing the coffee house to close?"

"No. I have reconsidered. It is a worthy enterprise, one that is important to you and, as such, important to me as well."

She stared at him, her throat aching with feeling as his words sank in. "You would do that for me?"

"You are to be my duchess." Earnest eyes held hers. "It is my duty to protect you and to ensure your future happiness."

A kernel of relief began to unfurl in her chest. "It might work."

"Never underestimate the considerable influence of the Duchess of Hartwell." His eyes twinkled. "Adopting a philanthropic endeavor is all the rage among the *ton*."

She turned it over in her mind. "Your solution allows for the coffee house to remain open while also protecting my friends' good names."

"I shall make certain of it," he said. "You will be at the

height of fashion. Everyone will talk about how clever you are. They'll scramble to find their own pet cause."

The weight in her chest eased a bit. It could work. It might save her from the earl. But at what cost to Hart? "It is too much to ask of you."

His dark brows drew together. "Nonsense."

"It does not change what is between us." *Or isn't between us.* "I don't wish to have a husband who does not esteem me."

His eyes widened. "Of course I esteem you."

"You find my morals to be so lacking that you anticipate that I shall be an unfaithful wife." Her defiant tone challenged him to dispute her. "You have made your disdain for my character quite clear."

"The truth is that I have wanted you from the moment I first laid eyes on you."

She understood how he wanted her. "Like a man wants a strumpet, not with the care one feels for a wife."

Hart's face flushed. Taking her hand in his large, masculine grip, he directed her to a bench. "You are very direct, so I will not dissemble with you." He urged her down beside him. "I not only welcome the idea of possessing you in every way, I hunger for it."

She'd been right. Tears blurred her vision. She rose, but Hart's warm strong hand clasped hers, preventing her from leaving.

"The truth is also that I believe you will make a fine wife and mother," he continued. "I admire your strength of character. You have a keen mind and sharp sense of humor that I should like to see in my offspring."

"Truly?" Her chest swelled with feeling and tears of a

different sort threatened now.

He nodded, a devilish glint entering his eyes. "Although you can be tiresomely stubborn, conversing with you is far more enjoyable than with anyone else of my acquaintance."

Delight jolted her. He preferred her company to anyone else's. She gazed into the gardens, processing his response. He esteemed her as a person. And there was certainly plenty of passion between them. She'd already experienced his heady desire for her. Perhaps he did not find her beautiful and he certainly hadn't given her his heart, but they still had more common ground between them than in most society marriages. She squelched a lingering pang of disappointment. She had hoped for more, for love, yet Hart had been honest. He'd made no empty pronouncements about love. And he'd pledged not to be unfaithful.

She would be married to a man whose self-assuredness and raw charisma appealed to her. Oh, he could be infuriating, but it dawned on her that she liked the challenge of talking to him, of being able to match wits with him. He had undeniable charm and an appealing tendency towards easy laughter. Marriage to the Duke of Hartwell promised benefits that outweighed any negatives.

"Thank you for your candor." She chose her words with care. "If that is truly how you perceive our future, than I would be unwise to object to such an arrangement. It seems as though we might suit after all."

A delighted grin opened up across Hart's face. "Well then, that appears to settle the matter. Shall we?" He rose and offered his arm. Willa stood and placed her arm in the crook of his elbow. She felt a warm satisfaction when he placed his other hand somewhat possessively over hers, making her feel safe and treasured.

"Tell me more of India," she said as they walked. "Have you visited the Taj Mahal?"

His eyes warmed. "My future duchess is full of surprises. What do you know of the Taj Mahal?"

"I find India fascinating. There are many stories in the *Times* recently about the East India Company's charter being renewed."

"Not only is my betrothed wife undeniably lovely, but she has a curious mind as well."

Willa's heart beat a little faster. "Stop making sport of me." She gave his arm a light tap. "You are fortunate to be able to travel to whatever faraway lands capture your fancy." It was something an unmarried lady in her position could only dream of.

"Very well. The Taj Mahal. It is in the city of Agra. They say it is a tribute to lost love. A mogul emperor built it as a testament of love to his favorite wife. She died bearing their fourteenth child." He paused and looked at her. "Perhaps I shall build a monument to you after our first child is born."

Their first child. She couldn't help but smile at the thought. What a romantic notion. "Have you seen it?"

"The taj mahal? Yes. It is also their tomb. They are buried there together." He stopped and gave her a thoughtful look, the sun's shadows falling across the sharp lines of his face. "It reminds me of you."

"Me?" Was he comparing her to a building? "Strong and stable perhaps?"

He laughed. "Hardly. The Taj Mahal is made of a white marble unlike anything you've even seen. When the sun shines down on it, the place literally glows." His eyes lingered over her face. "You have that quality. You truly seem to radiate from within. It is most enchanting."

The unexpected caress of his voice and intimacy of his tone made Willa's stomach tingle. He tilted his head down toward her and brushed his lips against hers. This kiss was hot, gentle and excruciatingly intimate. Her lips, soft and welcoming, parted for him and his tongue glided against hers in long tantalizing strokes. His intimate taste was warm and delicious, thoroughly masculine, and the impact of the kiss showered through her, leaving her weightless, as though she were both falling and floating.

"Oh, my lord, may I be of service?"

Recognizing the voice of Harry, the lead gardener at Camryn Park, Willa pulled away with a rush of horror. Beyond the hedgerow came Cam's answering voice.

"No, not at all, Harry." She froze, a cold rush of fear pumping through her veins. She couldn't see them, but their voices suggested they weren't far.

"I was boasting of our exceptional flower garden to our guests." Cam's voice sounded closer now.

"We seem to have a knack for getting caught in compromising situations." Frustration and dark amusement warred on Hart's flushed face as he tucked a loose tendril of hair behind her ear. "Although I shouldn't mind being forced to push up the wedding."

Chapter Ten

Willa slipped into the library for a few moments of solitude, reluctant to join the other ladies who were gossiping and doing needlework in one of the public rooms. She settled into a comfortable chair by the fire and opened her book. It wasn't long before a short rap on the door interrupted her.

The door pushed open and Hart sauntered in, his eyes going to the book in her lap. "I thought I might find you hiding in here. Wollstonecraft again?"

Smiling in welcome, she nodded and put the book aside as he approached. The duke wore a linen shirt open at the neck, revealing a dusting of small dark curls. His muscular thighs were gloved in fawn breeches.

He came to stand in front of her chair, causing her pulse to ratchet up. "Wollstonecraft was quite the adventurer. She had children without the benefit of marriage. Lived with the man she loved." He bent closer, placing a hand on each armrest, his face just a hair's breadth from hers, his eyes like black velvet. "Tell me, Willa, are you adventurous?"

She swallowed, her nerve endings enthralled by his closeness and the clean masculine smell thickening the air.

"Wollstonecraft speaks of a woman's passion being like that of a man's." His eyes glowed. "Do you agree?"

"I cannot say I have fully experienced a man's passion," she said, feeling decidedly lightheaded. "Or my own for that matter."

Hart's eyes flashed in a way that made desire pool at the bottom of her belly. "I will endeavor to change that, my dear. We will have to mount a full exploration."

The back of Willa's neck prickled. He lowered his lips on hers, loving her mouth with light teasing kisses. She parted her lips to receive him. His tongue stroked inside with a seductive, flirtatious rhythm. Willa felt her skirt being lifted and then Hart's warm hand on her bare thigh at the top of her stocking. She froze.

"Are you willing to fully explore a woman's passion?" He watched her face as his finger skimmed the top of her thigh. "Solely in the interest of scholarship, of course. To test Miss Wollstonecraft's theories."

Heat flushed through her. How was it possible that she ached for his touch—down *there* of all places? "Perhaps when we are married—"

He chuckled against her ear and it rippled through her. "Not a forward thinking answer at all. What would Miss Wollstonecraft say?" His tongue slid inside her ear. "Tell me to stop and I shall." Willa closed her eyes, captive to the sensual uproar raging inside her, unable to bear the thought of him stopping.

He obviously took her silence as permission to go

forward. Straightening, he strode to the door and threw it shut. He pushed a heavy wooden table up against it. He turned and looked at her with gleaming eyes. Striding over, he lifted her without warning, carrying her to the table that now barred the door. He sat her on it, his lips coming down on hers.

"Now I am quite compromised," she murmured through his kisses.

"You shall be thoroughly so once I'm done with you." His fingers feathered along her inner thigh. Willa reflexively squeezed her legs together.

"Open your legs," he said softly, licking her ear, making her tremble. "Do not deny me." His lips came back to hers, consuming her again. His hands gently pushed her legs apart while his fingers still moved enticingly along them.

Willa's heart thumped through her body. Closing her eyes, she leaned back, relaxing her legs as the insistent throbbing between her thighs grew all encompassing.

Hart's unrelenting lips, soft and hot, moved along her neck with caressing kisses. His fingers brushed her most intimate area. She stiffened, embarrassed by the dampness he must feel there.

"Not such an ice queen after all." He seemed delighted. His clever fingers probed her folds, his breath coming out in short hard bursts. "You are perfect." He knelt, shocking her by kissing her intimate area.

Startled, she pushed him away. "Hart, do you—? Is it—?" She couldn't seem to form a coherent thought.

"Let me love you here, Willa," he said, kissing her there again. She bit back a scream of shock and pleasure when she felt the moist probing of his tongue moving lightly up and down along the length of her womanhood. He paused before delving his tongue inside of her. An intense tremor rocked her. She shivered and tried to move away from the delicious intensity, but Hart caught her, holding her hips as his tongue latched onto a spot that seemed to have a million nerve endings.

"You are so beautiful," he said huskily, his warm breath puffing against her intimate folds. "No other man will ever touch you like this."

"No," she panted, her womb convulsing with pleasure. She could hardly believe he was touching her this way. "Never."

He rose to his feet—a wildness lit his eyes. Sliding his hands over her breasts, his deep, dark gaze locked on her face. He stroked and caressed her breasts, which had never felt so sore and sensitized, through the thin muslin of her dress. "You are mine and only mine."

"Yes." She leaned back on her palms, her body trembling.

An intense look flashed across the sharp planes of Hart's face. He eased down her bodice, baring her breasts. His breath caught as his hands moved reverently over them, cupping and massaging. He tweaked an aching nipple between his thumb and finger. "Say it."

But she could only moan in response.

"Say you are mine and only mine."

Her body arched up of its own accord, offering her greedy breasts to his insistent fingers. She could not imagine ever wanting anyone other than this man. This man who touched her as though he knew her every secret desire. Her future husband. "I am yours and only yours, forever."

He bent and took a nipple into his mouth, sucking hard.

Shc bucked at the sensation, bringing her hand to his head, pulling out the ribbon that held his hair in a tidy queue. She ran her fingers through his loosened hair, reveling in its soft feel. He responded by sucking harder at her nipple, biting it gently. "To whom do you belong?" His voice sounded labored, almost guttural.

She writhed in a delicious agony. "I belong utterly and completely to you, Grey Preston, Duke of Hartwell."

He pulled his mouth away from her breast, his lips wet, his eyes glimmering with satisfaction. His loosened black hair enhanced the primal air about him. "Say it again."

She ached with desperation, but somehow found the words to tease him. "You are my lord, my master."

He laughed, his dark eyes gleaming. "As your lord and master, will you let me do with you as I please? Give you pleasure as I see fit?" Watching her face, his hand moved between her legs.

A painful ecstasy gripped her. She longed for his skillful fingers to answer the throbbing between her legs. "Yes. I am yours to do with whatever you desire."

"I should stop, but I find I cannot," he said in a hoarse voice. "Tell me this is what you want."

"Oh, yes please." She felt herself growing more desperate, hurtling toward some oblivion his touch seemed to demand.

"Show me," he demanded, his voice low.

She was in a haze again. "What? How — ?"

"Show me your passion, Willa. Prove Wollstonecraft's hypothesis about a woman's passion matching a man's. Show me you have the freedom to take your pleasure."

The knowledge that they were forever intertwined

emboldened her to accept his challenge. For the first time in her life, she felt completely safe and protected with a man.

This man.

Hart.

She relaxed and leaned back, giving herself fully over to him. Dropping the reserve that always guarded her innermost self, she surrendered her body completely to him.

He sucked in his breath. "You are as I saw you at the pond. Pure and unencumbered." He knelt before her again. "You are so beautiful. I want you to hunger for me as much as I yearn for you." He brushed a kiss on the inside of her thigh. "I want you to leave this encounter knowing there can never be another man for you."

He kissed her there again. She responded by crying out and arching her body, which was quickly careening out of control. The strokes of Hart's tongue became hard, deep, and relentless. Willa rocked with him, her entire being coiling up with tension. They moved together, lost in each other as though nothing else mattered. The library echoed with the sounds of their lovemaking, her soft moans as his mouth loved her and his fingers coaxed her to fulfillment.

Willa cried out in surprise when her release came, as bits of light and unfathomable pleasure exploded within her, tremors of bliss shimmering out to her limbs. When she came back to herself, Hart was kissing her. He lifted her, their lips still melded together, and carried her across the room. He settled her on his lap, lowering her skirt as they sank down in the large chair Willa had been reading in. They clung to each other in silence for a few minutes.

After a time, Hart smiled with lazy satisfaction. "I daresay we did Miss Wollstonecraft's theory proud."

• • •

Willa stood at her work table in the solarium, concocting a new brew she'd been thinking about for several days. Mixing the leaves, she exhaled a calming breath, grateful to lose herself to the endeavor. For a time, at least, it quieted her mind and pushed her troubles far away.

Although the situation with Hart had resolved itself in a most pleasing way, the earl still needed to be dealt with. She shook Augustus out of her thoughts. She'd worry about settling matters with him once he returned from Town.

She focused on the task before her. Hart's Indian tea had stirred her creative sensibilities. Its light flavor reminded her of a sweet wine. By blending it with a touch of green tea from China, she hoped to achieve a deliciously fruity taste. Inhaling the musky aroma, she considered how to best serve it. Cream would ruin the effect. Perhaps a touch of warm milk would be the perfect compliment.

Footsteps sounded in the hall. Expecting to see Hart, her heart quickened with expectation. Instead, Augustus stepped across the threshold.

Her heart contracted in her chest. "You've returned."

"Yes, I completed my affairs in town as quickly as possible." His eyes shifted to the teas on her work table. "Surely you are not still concocting those brews of yours?"

"It is for the guests," she said in a clipped tone. "My blends are always served at Camryn Hall."

He picked up a jar of tea and studied it in an absentminded fashion. "If it amuses you, I see no harm in it." He fixed a gaze on her. "It is well past time to finalize our betrothal."

She bit her lip at the sight of the earl handling her tea. She itched to tell him to remove his hands from it. Instead she said, "I am already promised to another."

His mouth pinched. "We have been over this."

She took the jar of tea from him and set it on the work table with a deliberate plunk. "I will not succumb to your demands."

He tilted his head while studying her, as though trying to determine what she was about. "You will allow your friends to fall into ruin with you?"

"No, the coffee house will be the Duchess of Hartwell's first philanthropic effort." The giddiness of triumph swept through her. "It will be all the crack. Everyone will want to follow the mode set by Her Grace."

"Do you think you can escape the stain of trade with that Bambury tale?" he asked, stepping closer to her, his voice rising.

"It is not a lie." She spoke in her calmest tone. "Hartwell owns the building and takes no coin from the coffee shop. Everyone will applaud our charitable endeavor."

"Don't do this." The words were urgent. "Not after all we have endured. This is our time, we must take it."

Discomforted by his proximity and familiar manner, she moved back from him. "Our time is long past."

He followed. "Willa, I must speak honestly and tell you what is in my heart."

"It is not my place to know what is in your heart."

"But it is." He took her hand and put it against his chest. "Feel that. My heart beats only for you. It always has. I love you, Willa. We finally have our chance. You mustn't squander it for some passing infatuation."

For an instant, she saw his vulnerability and glimpsed the companion of her youth. But the bond she'd once felt to Augustus didn't compare to the intense feeling and passion she felt for Hart. Just the thought of the duke's touch sent a shiver of excitement scurrying down her back. Her long-ago affection for Augustus now seemed flimsy and inconsequential by comparison. They'd been friends and neighbors. It had been quite natural for them to develop a flirtation. She smiled softly and eased her hand away from his. "I am betrothed, as you well know. Let us leave memories in the past where they belong."

"You love me." Stubbornness gleamed in his silvery eyes. "I see it in your face. You cannot marry another."

"I have fond memories of the boy you once were, but I do not love you and I realize now that I never did."

He stared at her in disbelief. "That cannot be true. You are my fate." Taking hold of her shoulders, he jerked her to him and crashed his lips down on hers.

She panicked, struggling against the hard, insistent lips pressed on hers, wet and demanding. It was like the inn all over again. His tongue slammed against the tight seam of her mouth, demanding entry. Her stomach turned, his perfume stung her nostrils, the smell of rosemary and almonds nauseating her. She wrenched away, ramming her hands against his chest.

"Stop, stop!" Her heart pounded her breath came out in short angry bursts. Any sentimental memories fell away.

Augustus smiled with satisfaction. "You must have felt the excitement." He put a finger to his lips. "I certainly did."

Disgust roiled her stomach. Her resistance excited him? "I feel nothing for you. Nothing."

"I suppose you think you love *him*," he said in a voice rich with scorn.

She blinked at him, awareness dawning. Did she love Hart? A joyous feeling took root in her chest. It all became so clear. "Yes. I do love Hart. I do." Where was he? She wanted to tell him immediately. She loved Grey Preston! Her heart seemed to lift out of her chest. The formidable burden of her dented reputation fell away, leaving her floating and feeling lighter than she had since that laughing girl had raced Augustus across the pasture.

"Or is it the title you want?" he said. "You aim high, my love. Most ladies would welcome the attentions of an earl."

"There is more to a man than his title." Her thoughts full of Hart, Willa smiled as a genuine feeling of delight engulfed her. "You would do well to remember that." The click of approaching footsteps sounded in the hall. "You really should remove yourself. Hart will throttle you again if he suspects you tried to force your attentions upon me."

"I'll go." Augustus grabbed her, forcing a hard kiss on her mouth before she could fight him. "For now. But this is not the end of it." He marched from the room, almost bumping right into Hart.

• • •

Hart zeroed in on Willa's flushed cheeks and flustered demeanor as soon as he brushed past Bellingham. Their glances met before Willa jerked hers away, dragging the back of her hand across her mouth.

Hart's eyes narrowed. "Are you all right?"

She turned away from him, busying herself with her tea

jars. "Yes, quite, thank you."

"Does he understand your betrothal to me stands?" Tension twisted into every one of his muscles. Perhaps she'd changed her mind and had decided to marry Gus after all.

That would explain the scene he'd witnessed through the solarium windows just moments ago when he'd stepped out for a cheroot: Gus grabbing her arm and Willa's radiant smile in return, a joyous expression impressed upon her lovely face. "Did you tell him you won't marry him?"

"I did." Willa placed a jar in the tea caddy and he experienced a fleeting satisfaction when he realized it was the one he'd given her.

"How did he respond?"

"He is not pleased." She exhaled a shaky breath, her back still to him. "But I think he will come to accept it as my final decision."

Her shoulders were stiff, hunched high into her neck. He laid gentle hands on them and turned her to face him. "Did he overstep?"

She looked beyond his shoulder. "No, of course not."

She was lying. Any idiot could see it. She couldn't even look him in the eye. Cold fury blasted through him. Retrieving his handkerchief, he held it out to her. "Perhaps you are in need of this."

Her enormous glistening eyes fastened on him. Finally. "What are you suggesting?"

"Did he force his attentions on you?"

"No. Please let us talk of something else."

"Even if something untoward happened, you would not tell me."

Willa sighed her resignation. "Yes, that's true."

Black rage pulsed through his body. "You seek to protect him because you love him still."

A tiny frown appeared between the perfect turn of her eyebrows. "Surely you comprehend after what occurred in the library that there is only one for whom I harbor feelings."

The rational part of Hart's brain believed her, but mad jealousy crowded out all sensible thinking. "After the library, I thought you understood you belong to me. Only me." His voice was frost now.

"I belong to no one." She studied his face. "Is that what happened in the library? Did you seek to mark me with your familiarity?"

"I gave you the pleasure he never could and yet you crave him still."

Fire flashed in her eyes. "You couldn't be further from the truth."

Hart clamped his hands on her shoulders, bringing his mouth down on hers. She tried to move away, but he held her firm. His insistent tongue demanded entry, his fingers dug into her flesh. She cried out, yanking her mouth away. Willa stumbled backwards, her eyes wide with anger and hurt.

Remorse slammed through him. *What the devil*. He'd never handled a woman roughly before. "My apologies." Spinning around in an angry daze, he stormed from the room.

• • •

Hart downed another ale. He wasn't sure if it was his third or fourth. He looked bleakly around the unfamiliar dark tavern. It stood in the village near Camryn Park, but felt a world away.

"Another?" asked the friendly barmaid, leaning over a little more than was necessary to refill his drink, treating him an excellent view of her best and biggest assets.

On another day, before Willa, he might have been appreciative. Not this evening. Now only one woman crowded his head, seeped into every bit of his being.

"You just passin' through, love?" asked the barmaid.

"Visiting Camryn Hall," he mumbled, bottoming out his drink. He tossed a coin on the bar. "Another."

She nodded, obliging him. "I'm not surprised you from the Hall." She topped off his drink. "I could tell you was one of the Quality."

Not in the mood for conversation, Hart grunted in response.

But she seemed not to notice. "Good people, his lordship and his family. The marquess is a just man. We was afraid when the old one died, but we needn't have worried. And the ladies are always helping the poor in the village."

He peered up at her. "What do you know of the ladies of Camryn Hall?"

"I suppose you're here for Lady Adela's betrothal." She wiped down the bar, nodding to a newly arrived customer. "A real beauty that one. We all wagered she'd marry higher than an earl's brother. T'was her sister we was expecting would end up in a Bellingham bed."

Hartwell's stomach flipped. "Why is that?" he asked mildly as he looked around the crowded tavern in a show of practiced disinterest.

"Young lovers they was, Lady Willa and the earl." She

winked conspiratorially. "Even brought her to the inn, he did. She made a fortunate escape by not wedding him, if you ask me. He's got a mean streak that one, likes to go hard on the wenches."

A furious pounding drummed behind his eyes. "Go on."

She shrugged her shoulders. "I done said too much."

In no mood for games, he tossed a coin onto the bar. Eyes gleaming, she reached for it. Hart clamped his hand down over hers, stopping her from scooping up the blunt. "Speak."

"It is said they took a room alone." Her eyes were fixed on the coin. "It was many years past, mayhap three or four."

Dread tingled the back of his neck. "Continue."

"You'd best ask one of the chambermaids at the inn. Ask for Dolly. I hear she's got quite a tale to tell."

Hart shot to his feet. "Where is this inn?"

It wasn't hard to find. The modest establishment stood on the outskirts of the village. It only took a few coins before the innkeeper led Hart to Dolly in the kitchen. Petite and pleasing to the eye, the maid's soft gold curls framed a pleasant face. She curtsied wide-eyed before he drew her out into the corridor for some privacy.

"I have need of information and will be very generous if your memory proves cooperative." He dropped a coin into her open palm.

Dolly's eyes rounded. "My lord, what is it you wish to know?"

"It is said the Earl of Bellingham brought a lady from a fine family to this establishment."

Understanding flashed in her eyes. "Aye, the Lady Wilhelmina," she said softly, looking around to make sure she was not overheard.

Pain stabbed his gut. "Are you certain it was she?"

She gave an earnest nod of her head. "Aye, there's no mistaking a beauty such as she."

Of course he'd heard the rumors, but that didn't stop him from feeling ill. "Did they take a room here?"

"Aye. The earl brought her up to it. I can show you the very chamber."

The thought of seeing the room roiled Hart's insides. Yet see it he would. It didn't take long to pay the innkeeper for a night's use of the chamber. He did not want to be rushed.

Dolly showed him upstairs and through a narrow corridor. She opened the door to a modest but clean room, bare except for a narrow bed, and a small wooden table and chair. He wondered if this room had looked the same when Willa had come here with Augustus. Was this where she had given herself to him?

He exhaled. "I suppose there is no telling what happened once they came here."

When Dolly hesitated, Hart dropped another coin into her hand. "Speak."

The wench lowered her eyes. "She came a maiden, but that is not how she left."

"How do you know that?" A sharp pain stabbed his gut. "It is a ruinous accusation you make."

"Nay, not I. The sheets tell the story. Proof that her virtue was no longer intact was left behind."

"Explain."

"She left her maidenhead on the sheets, she did. Marked with her innocence, they was. It wasn't a large stain but it were stubborn. It took the laundress a time to clean it."

His head swam. So there it was. The truth. In this very chamber Gus had stripped Willa naked and pushed himself inside of her. It explained why the whoreson acted as though Willa belonged to him. Turning to the bed, he pictured her lying there, smiling as she spread her legs, beckoning Bellingham into her.

Painful awareness of what had happened on this bed clogged his lungs and tore through his belly with such force he was at a loss of what to do with the enormity of it. Looking blindly around, he caught sight of Dolly standing in the doorway. She gave him an uncertain smile. Hart took in her modest curves and sweet countenance.

He dropped two coins on the bed and began to untie his cravat.

Chapter Eleven

Dolly closed the door and went to him, pulling off her simple dress before climbing into the bed. He dropped down beside her and pawed clumsily at her, burying his face in the warmth of her soft flesh, desperate to forget the woman who had bedded another man in this very place.

Willa had been here, taking another man's strokes just as Dolly prepared to accept his now. His heart boomed painfully against his ribs. Had she enjoyed it? Had she cried out in pleasure?

He stilled, realizing he did not have the heart for this mindless coupling with a stranger. What he truly craved, he could not have because there would be no release from the truth. Rolling onto his back with a heavy sigh, he stared at the ceiling. Willa's essence permeated everything for him now, ruining the pleasure of any other woman's body.

Misunderstanding his reluctance, Dolly murmured words of encouragement and moved her hand to the place between his legs. He flinched, self-disgust and regret filling him. Why was he here? Had he lost all honor? In a gentle motion, he set her hand away from him. "My thanks, love, but it seems I will find no satisfaction this evening."

"Is she your lady then?"

He felt strangely at ease with the sweet chambermaid. "I am not certain."

"There weren't no happiness in her when she left. Looked sorry, she did, after it was done."

Alarm shot through him. Propping himself up on his elbow, he turned to look at her. "How do you mean?"

"She ran away quick, she did, when it was done. There was tears."

"Did he force her?"

Dolly shook her head, rising from the bed. She pulled on her dress. "I cannot say. But the earl has a certain reputation."

"Meaning?"

"Hurting girls, humiliating them, it is the way he derives pleasure from the act. The village maids who bedded him say it is the only way he can...perform."

Nausea swirled low in his belly. "You think he hurt her?"

"Maybe not. She is a lady, after all. There weren't no screaming. No signs of trouble inside the room once the earl took his leave. Except." she paused.

"Yes?"

"There was broken glass when I came to clean up. The earl paid for the damage. But the rest of the chamber 'twas fine."

He watched Dolly dress, taking in the sight of her slender, petite form, inadvertently comparing it to the elegant, luscious woman he truly hungered for. Hart rose and righted his clothes, anxious to be as far away from this bed and its thwarted dreams as he could manage.

He dropped a light kiss on Dolly's warm soft cheek and closed another coin into her hand. "Thank you, love. I bid you good night."

· · ·

Willa wasn't sure what woke her. Perhaps he shifted or made a noise. Whatever it was, she became aware of Hart's presence the moment she opened her eyes. Sitting up in bed, she peered around the curtain her maid hadn't bothered to draw.

He sat sprawled in a chair by the escritoire, his hips pushed forward, legs splayed apart. His white shirt was wrinkled as though he'd just come from his bed. Firelight flickered over his sharp-edged features, revealing the deep, black hollows of his eyes. His hair, usually so controlled and immaculate, hung loose, the inky strands strewn about his shoulders in a way that gave him a savage kind of grace.

Where had he been? Why had he come? She'd been so anxious to share the wondrous discovery that she loved him. For her, the library had been about love and complete trust in each other. But earlier today in the solarium, Hart had made it something less pure and honest. Tomorrow evening they were to become betrothed. Dread clutched her stomach. Perhaps he'd come to tell her he'd changed his mind.

"It is no use."

"What is?" Reaching for her dressing gown, she stood and pulled it on. "What are you doing in my chamber?"

"It is of no use." He repeated as though he hadn't heard

her.

Alarmed at the desolation she heard in his voice, she went to him and knelt between his spread legs, placing her hand just above his knee. He stiffened at her touch. "What is it, Hart?"

"It doesn't matter what happened in the past because I find I can't let you go." He fingered a strand of her hair, the action making her scalp tingle with lazy pleasure. "I know that for certain now."

She knew who he meant. "I don't want him." She rested her chin on the hand on Hart's thigh, a familiar rush of desire coursed through her. He smelled of drink and cheroots and the sweaty, earthy essence of something else she couldn't identify.

"I will kill him if I ever learn he harmed you against your wishes." His black gaze held hers. "Or if he ever touches you again. You belong to me now."

It felt like a rock clogged her throat. "If you have so little faith in my honor, why do you take me to wife?"

"It is myself that I have so little faith in." He put her away from him almost as though she were fragile and could break. Rising, he went to stand before the fire and spread his arms wide, as if to usher heat into his body. "Perhaps I judge too harshly, hunger too deeply, and love too strongly."

She stood, feeling a glimmer of joy. *Love too strongly*. He loved her? If so, it didn't seem to be as joyful a revelation to him as it had been for her. "I don't understand."

He turned and smiled but it was wistful. "I think you do, Willa."

He spoke of love. But she could discern the lack of trust in his eyes. She stiffened, the heavy ache of disappointment bearing down on her chest. "Let us just end it here. If you think me a strumpet who would give favors anywhere she sees fit—"

"You are not a strumpet, but I was with a whore earlier this evening. I bought and paid for her and I was going to take her to bed and try to forget you."

She recoiled at the thought of him coming to her from another woman's bed. Comprehension sickened her when she realized it was likely the whore's scent that still clung to him. "If you seek to disgust me with your lewd behavior, you've succeeded admirably well. Please leave me."

"I will never let you go just as surely as there will never be another woman for me." He spoke matter-of-factly, as though resigned to the bond between them. He came to stand before her and traced his finger along the planes of her face. "Don't you see? It's not you I don't trust. It is myself and these passions that render me blind with jealousy and mad beyond all reason."

He went down on both knees before her in a stunning gesture of supplication. Dukes knelt before no one but royalty. He wrapped his hands around her waist and buried his face in the soft plane of her belly. Despite her fog of jealousy, anger, and confusion, Willa couldn't stop her hand from coming up to comb her fingers through Hart's long, loose hair. Even now, she still found it impossible to keep her hands off of him. But his strange mood confused her. It did not seem possible their argument in the solarium would have this effect.

He laid a cheek against her stomach. "If this is love, it is a confounding thing, Willa. Whatever it is, I would have you to wife. Even if you do not feel the same way."

Her heart expanding, she sank down to face him before the rational part of her mind could stop her. She cradled Hart's face in her hands, taking in the sharp lines she'd come to covet. He brought his lips to hers, intense and probing. Willa opened her mouth to him, inviting whatever emotion uncoiled from deep within him. He clasped her to him and she lost herself against the hardness of his body and the soulfulness of his mouth on hers. They clung to each other, trying to drown out the emotional chaos engulfing them both.

. . .

The day of the ball broke with a chill in the air. The overcast sky did little to dull the anticipation inside Camryn Hall. This evening's ball would be the highlight of the house party. Servants scurried about, dusting and preparing the ballroom for the evening, laying out flowers and candelabras.

Willa had already dressed for the ball when Clara entered her chamber to deliver a missive from Hart.

Meet me in the Rose Salon now ~ H

He'd chosen a rarely-used room where they were unlikely to be discovered. What was Hart about? She remained perplexed by his mystifying mood last evening, but there was no denying the deep emotion and passion that lay between them. Although much remained unresolved, she now looked forward with great anticipation to becoming his wife.

"The valet of one of the guests delivered it," Clara told

her as she moved about, straightening the clothes strewn across the dressing room floor. "Said you should receive it immediately."

Willa glanced at herself in the mirror. Her pale blue dress contrasted nicely with her dark hair. Her eyes sparkled with anticipation. Satisfied with what she saw, Willa slipped out into the hallway and made her way to the Rose Salon.

With final preparations in full swing for the evening, Camryn Hall was a flurry of activity. Bouquets of flowers seemed to cover every available surface, their sweet scent saturating the air. Maids moved about lighting the myriad of extra candelabras which had been set up, while footmen hurried along taking care of other final details before the arrival of the first guests.

Willa left the bustle behind as she drew closer to the Rose Salon. They rarely made use of this part of the house so it was quiet and isolated, and a chill nipped the air. She slipped into the room, relieved to see a fire blazing in the fireplace. Two large high-backed chairs faced the fire. She headed towards one to warm herself while awaiting Hart's appearance. A chilling voice came from behind her. "Willa, my dear. I'm delighted you've come."

Willa spun around to find Augustus leaning in the door frame. He advanced into the room and closed the door. The move was highly improper and put her reputation at risk.

"Why do you look so surprised, my dear? Were you expecting someone else?"

What did he want? "Did you follow me here?"

Augustus appeared relaxed and confident. Foreboding shot up her spine. She tried to comfort herself with the knowledge Hart was on his way. Yet, an immediate and instinctive urge to escape Augustus propelled her toward the door. He seized her arm as she passed, swinging her around to face him.

"Oh no, Willa sweet," he crooned, his breath hot and humid on her cheek. "You go nowhere until it's done."

"Unhand me." She struggled to keep her voice cool, despite the anxiety welling up inside of her. "The guests are soon to arrive."

"I will have you, Willa, right now, right here." The earl's silvery eyes were almost feverish in their brightness. "I will compromise you so thoroughly and so publicly this time that no man will have anything to do with you. Not even your duke."

Bile rose in her mouth and her knees went soft. "Augustus, the Duke of Hartwell is on his way. Release me and we shall both forget this folly of yours."

He smiled as though genuinely amused. "He is not coming, Willa. It's just you and me, now and forever more."

Realization dizzied her. "You sent the note."

"Always the clever girl." He ambled over to the door and locked it before slipping the key into his pocket. "My valet will lead a large and varied group to find us. First, they'll find the door locked. Then imagine their surprise when they discover us in a state of undress when we finally do let them in."

Horror weighted her limbs. "It won't work." But she knew it could. And probably would.

"I've made certain the group that finds us will include some of society's least discreet matrons."

"Hart won't believe it. He'll destroy you."

"Are you certain of that?" He stalked a circle around

her, his eyes riveted on her face. "Have you never wondered why you receive no quality proposals? They all know you are mine. I've made certain of that."

"Yes, you certainly did," she said bitterly.

"Except for Hartwell. I suppose his time in India placed him beyond the reach of rumors. However, as you've already allowed him certain liberties, discovering our little tête-à-tête will confirm his likely suspicions that you routinely share your favors with more than one gentleman."

Willa's stomach heaved. This couldn't be happening, not when a life with Hart lay just within her grasp. She prayed for help, searching her mind for a way out. She must convince Augustus not to want her.

"He's touched me everywhere. There is no place on my body that does not belong to him." She burned a gaze into his face. "I'll never stop hungering for Hartwell. Even as your wife, I shall invite him to share my bed. He will do as he pleases with me, whenever he chooses. I will cuckold you every chance I get. You will never be certain whether the babes in my belly are yours."

He gave a quiet laugh, the puff of humid breath sliding over her skin. "How sad that your undeserved reputation would lead many to believe you are capable of such deceit." He stopped, his lips almost brushing her ear as he spoke. "But you forget that I alone truly know you. Your honor would not let you do such a thing. Once you are my wife, you will not betray me. We both know it."

"He loves me," she insisted, sounding more certain of it than she felt. In truth, Willa had a sinking feeling Hartwell would not want her after tonight.

Augustus reddened. "Do you think he'll desire you once

he knows my seed is in you?" he snarled. "Did I mention that your exalted duke will be among the lucky group who discovers us?" Willa felt as if all of the air had been sucked out of the room. She couldn't draw a breath. "Or I could just make you my mistress after I ruin you here tonight," he said. "I doubt the great duke will be interested in my whore once I am done with her."

"Actually, you are wrong," said a strong masculine voice. "I would want Lady Wilhelmina any way I could get her."

Chapter Twelve

Hart's tall, black-clad frame rose from one of the two high-backed chairs that faced the fireplace. Relief swamped her. He'd been here all along, hidden in the large chair facing the flickering flames.

Augustus blanched. "What are you doing here?"

The duke's menacing grimace made the back of Willa's neck tingle. "There is nothing I would not do to have her with me. I would cut off my arm." He took a casual step toward Augustus. "More importantly, I would tear off your arm to have this lady by my side."

Augustus stepped back. "How did you find us?"

"I was suddenly overwhelmed by an uncontrollable desire to see the Rose Salon." Hart bared his teeth in a snarl-like smile. "An interesting coincidence, don't you think?"

Augustus drew himself up. "Shall we settle this as gentleman" —his voice wobbled— "or may I depend upon you to revert to your innate savagery?"

"A duel? No. Nor will I give you the basting you so sorely deserve." Hart leaned into Augustus, cold fury infusing the jagged edges of his face. "You will not escape quite so easily this time. Your reckoning shall come, but at a time and place of my choosing." He offered his arm to Willa, which she gladly took, her legs shaky with relief. "For tonight, however, my beloved and I shall become betrothed. And her sister and your brother will enjoy this evening despite your best efforts."

There was a rap on the door followed by a man's voice. "Hello, hello?" he called out. "Is anyone in there?"

Hart's dark brows drew together in amusement. "Ah, the big denouement." He chuckled, placing his hand over Willa's as it lay in the crook of his arm. "Only it does not quite end as you'd planned. Open the door, Gus."

· · ·

 Hart's chest flared as Augustus slipped away a few minutes later, eagerly joining the group of guests on a tour of the lesser-known parts of the house. He somehow resisted the urge to tighten his hands around the whoreson's neck until he'd squeezed the life from him. Then he noticed Willa was shaking.

His heart clenched as he took her hand. "Are you well?" Her skin felt cold beneath his. "Come, sit." He drew her to the chair in front of the fireplace, kneeling down before her, using his hands to warm the delicate lengths of her fingers.

Willa's white face looked into the fire. "I just need a moment to collect myself." She turned her gaze to Hart, her velvety chocolate eyes huge and wondering. "How did you know where to find me?"

"Do you think I would let Bellingham roam Camryn Park unchecked? I've had him watched," Hartwell explained. "So when his little note was delivered, I was among the first to know."

A shudder coursed through her. "When I think of what could have happened—"

A black cloud of fury engulfed him. "I shall deal with him later."

"You must know the full truth of it before our betrothal is announced."

His gut quaked at the thought of hearing the truth from her lips. It somehow made it too real. He'd already battled long and hard to put images of Augustus bedding Willa out of his mind.

"No." He rose to his feet. Willa caught his hand with both of hers from where she sat and laid her forehead against it. Hart stilled, standing before her, his hand on fire from the satin feel of her cool porcelain skin.

"Ask me."

A suffocating feeling engulfed him. He shook his head. "No."

"You speak of love. Offer it fully then." Releasing his hand, she rose and moved behind the chair she'd been sitting in. His eyes fastened on the delicate femininity of her hand resting atop the high back of the chair. "Ask me for the truth so we can both be free of it."

She was resplendent in her sky-colored ball gown, which complimented her dark eyes, tumbling curls, and glowing complexion. He'd never laid eyes upon a more exquisite woman, inside and out.

Ask me.

He had a million questions. And none. Lord help him, he wanted her, loved her without reservation. He should spare her the indignity of his questions. But he had an overwhelming, unquenchable urge to know. "I will ask you once and then we shall never speak of it again."

She nodded, waiting with quiet dignity for him to continue.

His breath scraped across his lungs. "Did he force you?"

"Force me?" Willa's face betrayed her confusion.

"The inn."

Anxiety and shame showed in the comprehending look that washed over her face. She had a death grip on the chair, her knuckles white with the exertion.

"I don't sit in judgment." He tried to reassure her. "I have not lived the life of a saint."

"That is most generous." A faint smile appeared on her pale face. "But standards of decorum are considerably more lax for gentlemen than for ladies and well you know it."

He brushed the soft velvet of her cheek with the back of his hand. "I just seek reassurance that you were not forced."

She closed her eyes and leaned her cheek into his hand. Then she opened her eyes and looked directly into his. "No, there was no force. I went to the inn of my own silly, youthful volition. Nothing was forced upon me."

He dropped his hand. Black jealousy snaked through him. She had been willing. Willa let Bellingham touch her, bed her. Hart could hear the chambermaid's words. *She entered an innocent, but that is not how she left. She left her proof of her maidenhead on the sheets.* He spun away from her, stumbling towards the window, trying to calm the storm raging in his head.

She came to stand beside him, gazing out at the day's last remnants of light. "Augustus convinced me that once I'd been compromised, our parents would allow us to marry. But the old earl was looking for a much bigger dowry to help meet his debts." She laughed without mirth. "A girl's silly romantic notions result in her downfall. It is an old and unoriginal story."

The images crashed through Hart's mind: Bellingham grunting over Willa, driving himself into her softness, his greedy mouth tasting her lush lips, hands roaming over the expanse of her curves. And she had been willing. Perhaps even craved it.

Utterly and completely compromised.

Squeezing his eyes shut, he tried to blast the lurid images from his mind, attempting to calm himself by reasoning out his reaction. After all, he'd learned nothing new. Hart exhaled in a deliberate manner and forced the tension from his shoulders, restoring some semblance of calm. Clarity seeped back into him. He still wanted her. Despite everything. He'd told Bellingham the truth. He would take Willa any way he could get her. Even if she were no longer untouched.

He turned to Willa and took her hands into his. It dismayed him to feel her skin had again lost its warmth. "Thank you for your frankness. We shall never speak of it again."

Two tiny lines appeared between her eyebrows. "Surely you can't mean to continue with this betrothal."

"I find myself growing quite attached to the idea of having you at my side in my dotage." Hart turned her hands over, brushing a tender kiss on the inside of each blue-veined wrist. "I won't allow you to cry off that easily."

"I will tell Cam everything." She blinked, tears shining in her eyes. "He's well aware I've little honor left to save. You deserve a duchess worthy of your admiration and affection."

"Such a lady is before my eyes." He couldn't bear to see her exquisite face ravaged by anguish. "Cease this nonsense and kiss me."

He brought his lips to hers, loving her gently as though she were a mortally wounded bird he could breathe back to life. She slipped her arms around his neck, the unbearable sweetness of her trust in him making his chest swell with emotion.

He surrendered to it all—his love for her, their future together, and the inescapable truth that he could no more part from this woman than he could stop the sun from rising in the eastern sky or the tide from coming in with the moon.

• • •

"You are truly a beautiful bride," Mother proclaimed with a maternal satisfaction. She looked at her daughter's reflection in the mirror. Adela and Matilda stood behind her, murmuring her approval.

Willa had Hart to thank for the exquisite wedding dress. He'd had the fabric for it delivered not long after they'd all returned to Town. The dress turned out more beautifully than she could have hoped. It had a high waist with a simple under dress made of a light white organza. The layer of delicate white silk lace that topped it took Willa's breath away. The intricate netting had a touch of silver in it, casting a luminescent sheen when it caught the light. Willa's abundant chestnut curls were put up, with delicate strands of silver interwoven into them. Looking at herself today, on her wedding day, Willa actually did feel beautiful.

The month since the announcement of their betrothal had passed in an astonishing whirlwind. Once they returned to London, Willa's mother had set the modiste immediately to work on a trousseau for the bride to be. Willa had not seen much of Hart. He'd called most afternoons, but they'd rarely been alone.

"It is time," Mother said, cutting into her thoughts. "The carriage has arrived."

Willa floated through the rest of the day in a dreamlike state. She saw Hart waiting for her at the altar as she entered the church. He wore black superfine with a soft gray waistcoat that complimented the silver threads in Willa's dress. His dark eyes flashed as she approached, the chiseled lines of his face sharpening. His magnetic presence commanded her toward him, his usual teasing demeanor now serious and unsmiling.

It was a small morning service and later Willa would barely remember saying the words that made her Hart's wife. The modestly attended wedding breakfast took place at Hartwell's Mayfair townhouse, her new home. Later, Willa would recollect the laughter and sense of general goodwill that permeated the air, the sounds of clinking glasses and people's chatter wafting throughout the main rooms and out into the small garden. There was Cam lifting his glass, leading a congratulatory toast, the pride and joy in her mother's face, and the barely concealed astonishment in the faces of others.

When the time came for goodbyes, Hart led Willa out

to the post chaise. They were to make their wedding trip to Fairview Manor, Hart's ancestral estate. The eyes of the more curious guests followed them, taking in their every gesture, trying to discern any words the duke exchanged with his new duchess. Hart handed Willa into the carriage, his hand giving hers a warm, gentle squeeze.

He settled into the carriage across from her and rapped on the roof, signaling the coachman to move on. Willa watched him, her heart moving faster. As always, his hair was immaculately tied back at the nape of his neck, emphasizing the sharp planes of his face. He settled back against the squabs and looked at her, and she thought she saw glimpses of joy in those midnight blue depths, although she couldn't be sure.

Her husband cleared his throat. "If we continue straight on without stopping, we should reach Fairview well after nightfall." He paused, studying her. "Of course, there is an inn I often use which is quite comfortable if you'd prefer to overnight along the way." He was politely giving Willa the choice of where she would prefer to spend her wedding night.

When she didn't answer immediately, he spoke again. "Unless you would find staying at an inn disagreeable."

Discomfort twitched in her belly. Perhaps he thought consummating their marriage at an inn would resurrect old memories. Of another inn. With another man. Willa's ears burned at the thought. "Whatever you prefer."

"The rational course would be to stop at an inn." He smiled and she saw the heat in his eyes. "But I am not always given to rational thoughts when it comes to my new wife."

"As you please."

"Very well, then." Hart settled back in his seat. "We'll stop for rest and refreshment and to change horses, but I've instructed the coachman to complete our journey this evening."

Fingering the pendant of her necklace, she stared out the window. Of course, Hart would have difficulty putting her history with Augustus aside. But to have Augustus's presence felt here in the coach between her and her husband on their wedding day caused a pang of regret deep inside her.

She could feel Hart watching her. "You never looked more beautiful than today in your wedding dress."

"A bride could not help but look her best in a gown made of such exquisite materials. Where did you find it?"

"I did a little bartering with another shipper. The lure of sugar made him willing to part with some of his finest fabric."

"That was most fortunate for me."

"I didn't think you could look more beautiful but once I saw you in that dress I realized I was mistaken."

She winced at being called beautiful when she knew she was not.

Hart leaned forward. "What is it?"

Shaking her head to indicate it was nothing, she returned to the view outside her window.

"Oh, no you don't." Hart moved beside her and reached for her hand, and his clean robust scent stole over her. "You are not going to retreat into that icy shell. Tell me why a mention of your obvious beauty prompts this withdrawal."

Willa watched his hands play with her fingers, moving over the inside of her palm. Sensation jolted up her arm. "I am your wife now and, if nothing else, we have learned to deal honestly with each other."

He brushed a kiss on her temple, his hand still caressing hers. "Is it that I insult you by only referring to your physical beauty?" He fingered a tendril by her face. "Perhaps you would prefer that I compliment your beautiful mind instead."

Delicious warmth flowed through her limbs in response to Hart's light touches. "That would be more honest."

"How so?" he said.

"I shall warm your bed this evening and any other night of your choosing from now until death parts us. There is no need for you to invent untruths to turn me up sweet."

His face twisted in confusion. "What untruths are we talking about?"

"Really, Hart, it is not gentleman-like to make me utter the words aloud." She sighed. "We both know I am no great beauty. There is no need to pretend otherwise."

His caresses faltered. "I would think you are being coy, but I know that is not your nature."

"I would prefer for us to be honest in our dealings with one another," she said, her ears burning.

"My dear, the truth is that your physical superiority is obvious to everyone but you. How is it possible you do not know how lovely you are?" He looked at her with open appreciation and desire. "Your beauty leaves me breathless. I have to stop myself from saying it aloud every day so as not to appear the lovesick fool."

Beautiful? She knew it wasn't so. "I assure you yours is a unique perspective."

"Nonsense, there is not a man who sees you who doesn't want you, who isn't struck by how stunning you are.

It amazes that you aren't cognizant of it. Women far less beautiful than you are extraordinarily aware of their looks." His fingers skimmed the inside of her hand. "Every part of you is beyond compare. No one has lovelier fingers." Hart brought her hand to his lips and surprised her by taking a finger into his mouth. His tongue flicked over it and then suckled it.

An astonishing surge of longing jolted through her. Hart's clean masculine smell prickled her senses, heightening her awareness of the sharp turn of his cheekbones, the chiseled lips that toyed with her finger. She instinctively tried to pull her hand away but he held firm, watching her reaction as he tasted her, twirling his tongue around her finger. He took it deep into his mouth and then eased it back out, his mouth tight around her finger, the stroking back-and-forth motions leaving her breathless.

Hart's dark eyes gleamed while he watched, as the pressure built inside of her, in her chest and belly. And lower. She tilted her head back and closed her eyes, a soft moan escaping her mouth.

Then Hart stopped and she felt his firm hands at her waist. Willa's eyes flew open as he swept her from beside him to place her atop him. She straddled one of his taut thighs, the skirt of her dress pushed up, straining against her parted legs. Her breasts were at Hart's eye level.

He nuzzled the full swells above her neckline. "And these are the most beautiful bits of temptation." He slipped her bodice down, freeing them to his touch. His large hands cupped each breast. Hart's eyes darkened when the ripe pink nubs at their centers hardened under his gaze. "What could be more beautiful than that?" He bent his head to flick his tongue across each sensitive, aching tip. Willa gripped Hart's shoulders and cried out at the shooting sensation that made her body throb.

"No other woman compares to such perfection." He slipped his mouth over her breast, sucking on the point, drawing it out. Hart's hands moved under Willa's bottom, pulling her against his hardened male flesh.

Heat and want pulsing through her, she pushed her body against the evidence of Hart's desire for her, trying to answer the insistent throbbing between her legs. On instinct, she started moving in a rhythm up against his hardened body.

"Willa." He called out her name, surprise in his voice. She stilled, afraid she had done something wrong.

"No, don't stop. Whatever you do, don't stop." he said, pushing her dress up to her hips giving her more freedom of movement. His hands gripping her bottom, Hart helped her move. He put his head back against the squabs, growling with satisfaction.

They moved in tandem, ravenous and urgent. Hart's eyes fastened on Willa's face when she reached her peak, watching as her body seized and then shuddered.

Lost in the waves of shocking pleasure, Willa heard Hart cry out before burying his head in her breasts. Afterwards they were perfectly still. Willa kept her arms wrapped around Hart's neck. From her position still astride him, she laid her cheek on the top of his head, taking in the soapy smell of his hair. Hart embraced her, tilting to look up into her face.

"If you could but see yourself now, you would never doubt your appeal." Willa knew she must look a fright with her burning cheeks and tousled hair. Her parted lips felt swollen.

Hart brushed a kiss on her bare breast and Willa thought she heard him murmur, "Just beautiful." But it was hard to hear over the pounding of her heart.

· · ·

Despite the lateness of the hour, the household staff lined up to greet their new mistress when Hart and Willa arrived. They stood in a row, according to rank, in the massive entry hall where a crackling fire blazed in an immense white marble hearth. Hart introduced Willa to Mrs. Pearson, the housekeeper, and Digby, the butler. They in turn made the introductions of the household staff. Mrs. Pearson presented the maids while Digby introduced the footmen. The maids and footmen stood upright in a formal manner, sneaking curious looks at their new mistress. Willa smiled and repeated each name during the introductions, murmuring words to each person who stepped forward. Hart felt a surge of pride watching Willa glide down the line, elegant and self-assured, already every inch the duchess.

His mind went back to how she had moved atop him not so long ago, cheeks flushed against the pale perfection of her skin, her lips lush and swollen. His own body had reacted like an untried school boy. Despite not making love to her in the traditional way, he'd felt surprisingly sated after their encounter. He could not wait to bed her now, to finally make her his in every way.

He stepped forward. "Her Grace is fatigued. We shall retire." Willa's brows shot up at his interruption and then her cheeks flushed. He pulled her toward the stairs, anxious to show Willa to her chamber, the one that adjoined his.

"Really, Hart, what must the staff think?" she said once they were out of earshot.

"They will think I am anxious to bed my wife." Hart put one arm under Willa's knees, sweeping her off her feet and into his arms, carrying her up the stairs. "And they would be correct."

• • •

The duchess's rooms were enormous, making Willa's comfortable accommodations at Camryn Park seem modest in comparison. The bedchamber was swathed in pink velvet and silk. An opulent four-poster bed with thick carved posts standing sentry around it dominated the space. Willa's new dressing room was also generous in size and well appointed. Next to it was a door that Willa presumed connected to Hart's chambers.

"I'll expect you'll want to refurbish these rooms to your liking," Hart said, watching her.

Willa's gaze took in the details of her new rooms. "It's huge."

Hart laughed and kissed her cheek. "You are my wife now, sweetheart. Only the finest will do for the Duchess of Hartwell. Mrs. Pearson will send your maid up to help you change," he said, disappearing through the door that adjoined his rooms to hers.

It was too late for a bath to be made ready so Willa washed with a basin of warm water Clara prepared for her. Afterwards, she put on a new thin muslin nightgown and dressing gown from her trousseau. She pulled a nightcap over her unruly curls. Once Clara left, Willa could hear Hart moving around in his rooms. Muffled voices suggested his valet was still in with him.

She stood before the hearth, her heart racing, when she heard the adjoining door open. Hart loomed large in the doorway. His hair was loose, hanging in black strands around the uncompromising lines of his face. He wore a red satin dressing gown which fell open at the top, revealing a lightly muscled chest and a smattering of curly hair. Heat licked her skin at the sight of his bare calves, which were round with muscle and dusted with the same fine dark hairs.

Her mouth went dry. "I wasn't sure you would come since it is so late. It has been a tiring day."

He approached her and touched her cheek with the back of his hand. "Are you too tired for me, Willa?"

Yearning shot through her. She shook her head. "No."

Hart pulled her nightcap off, freeing her tousled curls. His eyes glittered with desire. "My first request as your husband is that you never wear one of these unfortunate contraptions to bed. Your hair is glorious. Let me see your glory."

Feeling shy, she ran her fingers through her hair to tidy it. Hart cradled her face in his large hands and kissed her slow and deep, tasting her with languid sweeping motions with his tongue, communicating a deep sense of longing and fervid need. Her legs dissolved beneath her. Feeling her waver, Hart caught her, pulling the length of her body up against his, her curves melding against his taut, muscled form. He took his time, exploring her fully, nibbling on her lips, leaving no part of her mouth untouched by his carnal exploration. Willa trembled under his touch, and waves of physical exhilaration lapped through her.

Taking her hand, he led her to the bed. He sat down on the side of it and pulled her to him so that she stood between his legs. He began to undo her wrapper. Jolted by his boldness, Willa flinched, her cheeks burning.

Surprise flickered in his dark eyes. "You know what happens in the marriage bed, Willa." It was a statement, not a question.

"Doesn't one usually put out the candles?" she managed to squeak out.

Hart smiled, drawing her wrapper off of her shoulders, allowing it to fall to the floor. "I am your husband now. I want to see all of you. Will you allow it?" He fingered one of her loose curls. Mounting desire overtook Willa's sense of modesty. Longing to see all of him too, she slipped her hands underneath his dressing gown to touch his bare shoulders. He felt hot, strong, and soft all at the same time. She pushed the cool, silky fabric away from his skin until it pooled at his waist, while her curious hands ran over the firm curves of his bare chest, over his shoulders and around his back. He stood, allowing his dressing gown to fall to the ground, leaving him completely bare to her gaze.

Willa's mouth watered. He was all sinewy muscle and hard curves. On the most basic level, she was fascinated, having never seen a naked man before. She ran her inquisitive hands down his sides and over the length of his body. She looked at the massive flesh between his firm thighs with a mixture of wonder and wanting. He was already hard and jutting.

"You can touch it," he said, the words both rough and tinged with a bit of desperation.

"Are you certain it's all right?"

He laughed, warm and deep within his chest. "Quite certain."

Willa reached down and wrapped her curious fingers around his male organ, stroking softly. Groaning, Hart reached down to pull Willa's thin nightgown over her head.

• • •

She stood naked before him, her fingers touching his aching flesh. Willa's luminous skin glowed in the candlelight, her wild curls cascaded around her shoulders, teasing at her lush breasts, their centers pink, lovely, and pert. She was so beautiful he ached with desire for her. Everything he wanted stood before him, his for the taking. He ran his hand over her shoulder and down to cup her supple breast, savoring its warm, succulent weight.

Had Bellingham touched her this way?

The traitorous thought invaded his mind. He dropped his hand, consciously shoving the thought from his head, trying to focus on the pleasure of Willa's fingers wrapped around his aching rod.

She looked at him, her eyes glistening with wonder and sexual excitement. "You are so soft and hard at the same time."

Had she done the same to Bellingham? Had she held him and stroked him the way she handled Hart now? He grunted, trying to thunder the thought from his mind. He bent to kiss her hard before tossing Willa up onto the bed. Crawling over her on all fours, he kissed her with unbridled passion, driving his hungry tongue into her mouth, tasting, delving, longing to possess her completely.

He reached down to the triangle between her thighs, his finger going to the center of her pleasure. *Had Bellingham done the same when he took her*? Hart shook his head and drove his tongue further into Willa's mouth, trying to eradicate jealousy's dark grip. He clumsily pushed Willa's legs apart and mounted her. Desperate to drive Bellingham's ghost out of his marriage bed, he buried himself deep inside her with a single forceful stroke.

He heard Willa gasp at the tearing sensation, letting out a small scream as she tried to push him off her to stop the pain. He stilled inside her, his mind confused and unable, at first, to grasp the undeniable truth of what Willa's body had just told him.

He'd felt her maidenhead.

She was a virgin.

Chapter Thirteen

Hart withdrew as gently as he could and tried to draw her into a protective embrace. She stiffened and rolled onto her side, inching away from him.

"Willa, I'm sorry, I didn't realize," he stammered, knowing how useless his words sounded, realizing the magnitude of his terrible mistake. Willa had entrusted herself to him and he had invaded her body like an animal. He should have gone slowly, prepared her tender flesh to receive him. Pangs of guilt and self-disgust swept through him. He touched her shoulder gently. "Willa—"

"Please, don't touch me," she said, her voice shaky. "I just need to be left alone for a moment. It…it was not what I expected."

His gut twisted. Grabbing a blanket from the foot of the bed, he spread it over her, shielding her naked body from his gaze.

He rose from the bed and pulled on his dressing gown.

His mind racing, he strode to the fireplace, unsure of what to do next. He shoved his hair away from his face and looked at Willa's shape under the covers. She looked small and frightened, curled up as though willing him to be gone. Because he didn't know what else to do for her, he went to the basin and wet a cloth. Returning to his wife, he knelt and she looked at him with large, unlit eyes.

Hart winced at the dullness he saw there. "Willa, I'm not going to hurt you, love." He spoke in a soothing voice. "I'm just going to help clean you up a little. I won't do anything you don't want me to."

Still looking dazed, Willa didn't protest when Hart drew up the blanket, uncovering only her legs and the triangle of dark fur between her thighs, while the rest of her body remained hidden by the blanket. She tensed when he began to wipe the red fluid from her thighs.

"There, love, almost done," he said, drawing the blanket over her lithe limbs to shield her again once he was done.

She finally looked at him. "Hart, you seemed angry when you did it… Is it always like that?"

"No, honey, no." He stroked her hair as self-loathing swamped him. "I was an idiot, an oaf. Please forgive me."

"I…I can't imagine doing that too often."

"I understand a woman's first time can be painful. I should have been more gentle. I didn't realize it was your first time." He regretted the words the moment they slipped out.

She stilled. "What do you mean?"

"Willa," he asked, his chest tight, "why did you lead me to believe you were no longer an innocent?"

"What?" Sitting up, she clutched the blanket tightly to

her chest, and waved off his stroking hand as one might swat a troublesome insect. "I did no such thing."

"You indicated that you and Bellingham—"

She stared at him in disbelief. Hart caught sight of the anger coming in behind the confusion. A part of him felt relief to see the old fighting Willa emerge. The other part began to realize just how colossal a mistake he'd made.

"The inn—" he said weakly.

Willa's face flushed with rising indignation. "You thought I allowed Augustus to *bed* me at the inn? Granted, I was an idiot to meet him there, but you must think me a total fool."

"The chambermaid at the inn said—" he began in his defense.

"The chambermaid at what inn?" Hart had a sinking feeling as comprehension dawned on her face. "You went to the inn? Why? To investigate me?" She looked around. "Drat! Where are my clothes?"

Hart picked them up, handing them to her.

"Thank you…" she said, years of etiquette kicking in before she could catch herself. "I mean…blast it. Turn around." He complied, listening to the sounds of her movements, the rustle followed by the slide of her nightclothes against her skin.

Willa faced him when she was fully clothed. "You went to the inn. When?"

"The night I saw you in the solarium with Bellingham, when we argued."

Her face scrunched up. "How would you even know to go there?"

"I was at the tavern, in my cups, and the barmaid there told me the rumor about you and Augustus and the inn."

She paled. "Go on."

"Willa, this isn't necessary."

"Tell me."

Hart sighed. "The chambermaid said you met him there. That you—" Another awkward pause. "That you…ahem… lost your innocence."

She reddened. "And you believed a chambermaid, a complete stranger?"

His head throbbed. "Well, in my defense, you never actually said you had not lain with Bellingham."

Willa's eyes widened. She opened mouth but no words came out at first. Then she found her voice. "Why would I even think to tell you such a thing? Have you taken complete leave of your senses?"

Hart blew out a breath. "The chambermaid took me to the room. She said you left blood on the sheets." His voice softened. "That you cried when you left."

Willa turned and paced to the bed, snatching up the red-stained cloth Hart had used to clean her. She hurled it at him. "Then how do you explain this?"

He caught it. "Willa, I know I was mistaken. I felt your maidenhead when I took you." He took hold of her arm, trying to calm her down.

She pulled away. "Please don't touch me," she said, shaking in the effort to control herself. She froze. "Wait. That was the night you came to my bedchamber, the night you said you'd been with a whore."

He avoided her gaze. The least he could do for her now was to be truthful. "Yes."

Suspicion gleamed in her liquid eyes. "Where did you find this whore?"

"Well, she wasn't what you could precisely call a whore," he said slowly, feeling like he was careening toward the edge of a cliff with no way to slow the momentum. "It was more like her side vocation."

"What does that mean?" she demanded.

"She is a chambermaid."

"A chambermaid?" Her voice rose in disbelief.

"Yes," he said, wincing inwardly. "At the inn."

"At the inn where you thought Augustus and I—?" Her face twisted with repugnance. "Not in the same bed that you believed that I…he—" she whispered, horrified.

Miserable, he sank down into a chair in front of the fireplace. "I fear so."

"So," she said, her voice shaking, "you believed I had no honor, and what we've discovered this evening is that it is you, Your Grace, who has no honor."

• • •

Willa awoke the following morning to a pounding headache. Looking around at the pink silk and velvet surroundings, it took her a moment to remember she was in her large, unfamiliar chambers at Fairview Manor. Thin shards of light streamed through a crack in the closed curtains. The door that adjoined Hart's chamber was slightly ajar but Willa couldn't discern any noises coming from the other side of it. She sat up and stretched, wondering how long she had slept. Dragging herself out of bed, she moved quietly so as not to awaken Hart. She was in no mood to face her new husband. The big dolt.

She focused instead on her first day as mistress of

Fairview Manor, intending to wash, dress, and get on with the business of being Duchess of Hartwell. Her marriage might be a disaster, but she had duties to attend to. She would begin by acquainting herself with her new home. She would meet with the housekeeper and go over the household accounts.

There was a polite tap on the door followed by a maid Willa recognized from last evening. The maid directed the footmen who'd arrived with warm water for Willa's bath.

"Pardon me, Your Grace. The duke called for your warm bath."

Hart strolled through the adjoining doorway, clad only in his crimson dressing gown. "Thank you, Vera." He turned to Willa, acting every inch the enamored bridegroom. "Darling, I called for the bath as soon as we awoke." He walked to Willa, draping an arm around her waist. "Vera, please bring a breakfast tray for us as well. And we are not to be disturbed after that." His commanding voice left no doubt who was master here. It was also full of implication.

Vera's mouth curved upward. Casting a knowing eye at the newlyweds, she kept her tone respectful. "Yes, Your Grace."

Willa flushed at Hart's insinuation and at the casual possessiveness of his firm hand at her waist. She willed herself to stay still, planting a small serene smile on her face. She could easily guess the gossip that would dominate the kitchens today, and she wouldn't compound matters by pulling away from Hart in front of a servant.

Hart tugged Willa closer to his side, tucking her against his masculine warmth. "After we bathe, you may change the bed clothes. My lady wife and I will take breakfast in my chambers while you do so. Oh, and Vera, Her Grace and I will take all of our meals in our chambers today."

Vera's knowing smile widened, but she avoided eye contact as she continued readying the bath. She kept her tone deferential. "Yes, Your Grace."

Willa struggled not to erupt in front of Vera. Hart was a bedlamite if he expected her to stay in these chambers with him for the remainder of the day. And if he anticipated a repeat of last night, a most unwelcome surprise awaited him.

The moment Vera finished her task and withdrew, Willa pulled away from Hart. "I will be taking my breakfast in the morning room," she said with cool disdain. "After that, I will ask Digby to give me a tour of the manor and then I plan to meet with Mrs. Pearson to go over the household accounts."

"You will breakfast in here with me, my dear wife." He dropped his tall frame into a chair by the hearth. "We are newly wed after all. What would the servants think if we were up and about so soon after the wedding night?"

Willa's chest squeezed. "I don't care what they think."

"Well, I do. I will not have you subject to any more speculation."

"Beg pardon?"

He sighed heavily. "Willa, as unfortunate as it is, there are widespread, unsavory rumors about your association with Bellingham. I heard them myself at Brooks, from men who are considered respectable." He crossed an ankle over his knee, baring a strong leg lightly dusted with dark hair. "I cannot allow that to continue. If we leave this room, it could suggest I was displeased with my new bride in some way. And given the rumors, it is not difficult to surmise what conclusion the servants will draw."

Casting a look at the stain of her maidenhead in the

unmade bed, she said, "And you begin my redemption by making certain the servants see the evidence of my innocence on the bed clothes."

Hart pushed to his feet and walked to her, brushing a tendril of wayward hair away from her face. Willa felt a familiar excitement at Hart's touch. Silently cursing her weakness, she moved away from him and toward the bath.

"So Willa," he continued, his eyes following her, "we will make every appearance of being the besotted newly-married couple. We are stuck together here in this chamber at least until the morrow. We will take all of our meals in here until the morning. Do you understand?"

The heat of anger rose in Willa. Hart meant to trap her in here with him when she craved to be as far from him as possible. What did he expect to do all day? She eyed the tub which had been readied for her. The steaming water would rapidly cool and she hated tepid baths.

"As you wish, Your Grace." Steeling herself against a natural inclination toward modesty and forcing herself not to rush, she unbelted her dressing gown and dropped the garment to the floor with a haughty disregard, revealing her bare body to his gaze.

His mouth dropped open. "By God, you are magnificent."

Taking her time, she stepped into the bath and sank down into it, the rush of warm water cradling her tingling body. Her challenging gaze met his. "I trust you won't force your unwanted attentions on me."

Hart cocked an eyebrow, his face darkening. Desire curled in Willa's belly and she hated herself for still wanting him after the disaster of last night.

"It is my right as your husband to bed you when I

please." He sauntered over to the bath, openly enjoying the sight of her bare body as he came to tower over her. "I could take you in that bath at this very moment and this time, you would enjoy it." His commanding tone made Willa stiffen. He reached down and she held her breath, waiting to feel his hands on her sensitized skin. But then a glint appeared in his eye and he reached beyond her, for the soap on a stool at her side. Straightening up, he dropped it into the water with a plopping splash. "However, I've never forced a woman and I don't intend to start now."

Fighting disappointment, Willa's defiant eyes held his gaze. She found the soap in the water and began to clean herself. She moved in an unhurried, methodical manner, cleansing the length of each arm, as though Hart were not watching her every move. The soap's rose fragrance filled the air.

Pointing a water-glistened leg out of the water, she ran both hands up her limb and then back down again. She repeated the motion with the other leg and still Hart did not move.

Hart's breathing grew louder when her hands glided over her breasts. She soaped them in rhythmic movements, with both hands, until their pink buds peaked. Heat gathered within her and a significant part of her wished the hands caressing her tingling skin were Hart's instead of her own.

His eyes clung to her every movement. Although he didn't touch her, her body alerted to his, and the impact of it heated her skin until she felt feverish. Still, she pretended to ignore him while giving each part of her tingling body the same concentrated attention. When her hands moved to her private place, she couldn't help flushing. Her body pulsed for him, especially there.

Hart groaned and spun away. "I begin to comprehend that this going to be a very trying day."

Willa leaned her head back on the edge of the tub and closed her eyes, her mouth curving in satisfaction.

• • •

The next day, she escaped him as soon as she could. Anxious to learn more about her new home, she asked Digby for a tour after a quick solitary meal in the breakfast room.

It was early, so the housemaids were still going about their morning tasks cleaning the grates and lighting the fires. She waved off the butler's apologies that all of the fires had not been lit before she left her chambers.

"Nonsense," said Willa. "It is I who should apologize for undertaking this tour so early in the morning." The housemaid snuck a quick look as she used a tinder box to light the fire, appearing amazed a duchess would think to apologize to servants. The rest of the staff was also busy, moving briskly about their work. Along the tour, Willa and Digby passed footmen cleaning and preparing the oil lamps and candles. Others were polishing the furniture in the principal rooms.

The portly, distinguished butler was polite and formal. As their tour progressed, Willa noticed the subtle but knowing looks from some of the servants. Even Digby's reproving looks didn't completely quell them. She imagined the stained bedclothes had done their work.

The size and opulence of Fairview Manor astonished Willa. Camryn Hall was large and gracious, but it seemed diminutive compared to her new abode. The second floor galleries alone were immense, running the entire length of the house. And Willa had never seen such gardens. They were meticulously maintained and encompassed well over seven acres, boasting dozens of different plant and flower varieties.

When their tour came to an end, Digby left Willa to explore the gardens on her own. Wandering through, she imagined herself spending a great deal of time in the garden on fine days. Looking at the variety of plants and blooms, Willa recalled her encounter with Hart in Camryn Hall's gardens. A fluttering heat rose in her chest as she remembered their shared passion and hunger that day. How different it had been from her wedding night.

Shaking the thoughts from her mind, she wondered whether Hart was awake yet. Being locked away together yesterday had been an ordeal. Willa had pointedly ignored him, turning to her books instead of letting Hart draw her into a game of chess or conversation. She'd played the role of adoring bride well enough when Vera brought their meals, but retreated back into her shell once they were alone again. Hart had been polite and solicitous, but she detected flashes of annoyance in him as the day wore on.

Walking at a brisk pace in the garden, Willa pondered Hart's revelations. Her initial surprise and outrage had receded, leaving a barrage of questions in their place. Outright doubts about her innocence were discussed openly at a gentlemen's club. By respectable gentlemen. It was beyond mortifying. Until now, bolstered by her family's support, she'd never fully comprehended just how ruined she was. That was no longer the case, of course. As Duchess of Hartwell, her new exalted station placed her above recrimination.

Still, Augustus' words reverberated in her mind. *They know you are mine.* He'd been so certain people would assume she belonged to him, even though she and the earl had not seen each other in years.

"There you are." Hart's avuncular voice sounded behind her. "Hiding out from me in the gardens?"

Willa turned to watch her new husband stride toward her. He dressed casually in a country style, his white shirt open at the neck, with snug brown breeches falling into slightly worn Hessian boots, unlike the gleaming black ones he usually donned. His midnight hair was tied back and he looked impeccable as usual.

Trying to harden herself against his appealing presence, Willa greeted him coolly. "I was just coming to find you."

His forehead lifted. "Oh? Dare I hope this means our wedding trip can continue in earnest? Let's lock ourselves away and I'll bathe you this time." A wicked gleam lit his eyes. "Naturally, I'll want to concentrate on all of the difficult-to-reach places."

Ignoring the heat that rose in her, she said, "What exactly was said about me at Brooks?"

Hart's eyes narrowed as if he expected another verbal assault from her. "Must we really get into this again?"

"This is not in reference to your crude assumptions about my character," she said. "I have a right to know what is being said about me."

"Very well. If you will do me the pleasure of walking with me, we can try to work this out together." He offered his arm.

Ignoring it, she moved ahead. "Fine, let us walk." She peered up at him, squinting against the sun. "What exactly are they saying about me at Brooks?"

To his credit, he did not hesitate to respond. "I believe the most cutting remarks alluded to the fact that you had been utterly and completely compromised by Bellingham."

She halted, stunned by the directness of the assault. "Those were the exact words?" She felt the blood drain from her face.

"I could not make them up," he said gently. "I, too, am interested to learn where these ruinous innuendos began. Although I already have a fair idea of their source."

"It must have come from Augustus himself," she said, more to herself than to him.

He took her hand in his and they continued walking. Lost in thought, she did not offer any resistance. "I gather Bellingham was not so bold as to say he ruined you outright," Hart said. "There is the question of the bloodstained sheets at the inn. Word of something so damning could have spread like the plague. Which I now believe is exactly what Bellingham intended."

A tightening sensation pulled across her chest. She stopped again and faced Hart. "I have not been completely honest with you about that night."

"You are under no obligation to enlighten me." He squeezed her hand. "I know everything about you that I need to. You owe me no explanations."

She paced away from him, wrapped up in memories, preparing to tell Hart what she had never before revealed to anyone. "He did ask it of me. Augustus said we could be together forever if we anticipated the marriage bed. He said our parents would relent to save our honor but, in the end, I could not go through with it. And when he kissed me, I found it beyond repugnant."

His face brightened. "Beyond repugnant?"

"At first, he wouldn't accept my refusal." She hugged herself as the memories shivered through her. "I was terrified and I fought him. We struggled and I remember slapping him." She turned to face Hart. "That's why your chambermaid saw me crying. I did leave in tears. But nothing happened beyond that kiss. Of course, I went to an inn alone with a man. I was behind closed doors with him. That alone is enough to ruin me. I thought you understood that."

A muscle ticked in Hart's jaw. "Bellingham comprehended it. Even though you could not go through with his scheme, he still made certain to get the results he wanted."

Realization washed over her. "He put the blood there to ensure the rumors."

"The chambermaid said there was a broken glass in the room."

"You think he cut himself purposely?"

"He wanted the story to be convincing. If he sought to keep you for himself, it was a small price to pay."

"That might explain why I received no worthy marriage offers," she said. "He ensured everyone would believe he took my innocence. He made certain no one else would want me."

"Except me. I wanted you no matter what occurred in the past." He brought her fingers to his lips. "Sometimes I wonder if I would be capable of the same level of deceit if it meant holding on to you forever."

Willa wasn't paying attention to him. She was still unraveling the mystery that had cast an unknown shadow over her for so long. "His father threatened to cut him off. So he decided to find a way to make me wait for him." She shivered. "It almost worked. The minute he came into the title, Augustus came for me."

"Unluckily for him, I managed to insert myself between the two of you."

Willa gave a harsh laugh. "There is a delicious irony to it. He sought to compromise me to keep me and he lost me because you ended up compromising me instead. It would all seem so silly if it did not have such dire consequences."

Anger bubbled up in her. Augustus had robbed her of so much. He had tried to control her destiny. "He cast this dark cloud over my life, even worse than I had ever imagined. I could do nothing to defend myself. Instead I flitted around like an idiot while everyone laughed at me behind my back." She looked up at Hart. "Who knows what course my life would have taken if he had not interfered?"

His features hardened. "Perhaps you've discovered you needn't have married me. Even I can see this marriage is an inadvertent result of Gus' scheming."

"I should like to return to Camryn Hall post haste."

A muscle in Hart's cheek ticked, revealing his surprise. "Your family is not there. They've already removed to town for the Season."

"I'll enjoy the solitude." The words were dispassionate, but her mind was in chaos. "I need time to myself to think, to sort all of this out."

"No." The words were strong. "People will talk if you remove yourself to your family's country seat so soon after the wedding."

"I am long past having a care for my reputation."

"I am not. I've only just begun," he said. "Which means I won't let you give the *ton*'s crows reason to gossip about you."

"Do you fear they'll think the rumor true?" she asked in a wintry voice. "That I tricked you into marriage with a fallen woman?"

"We will go to London as soon as you wish, but we shall go together." His granite tone brooked no opposition. "You won't have to suffer my company unduly. The house in town is large. For the most part, you can keep to yourself. However, we will make the necessary appearances in public to keep rumors at bay."

"You have no right to command me. For once, I want control of my own life."

"As your husband, I have every right to command you. However, I will do what I can to accommodate your need for independence. I shall place your dowry in a private bank account that will be yours alone to use as you see fit. You shall have complete autonomy."

"Except when it comes to my own person. Augustus will be in town. I wish to avoid him."

"The days of Gus Manning impacting where you go and what you do are over, my dear." He bent to skim a light kiss on her silken cheek. "And I promise you, his day of reckoning is close at hand."

Chapter Fourteen

Their return to London was welcomed by family and greeted with the expected curiosity on the social circuit. With the little Season just getting under way, the Duke of Hartwell and his new bride were much sought after guests. Willa accepted enough invitations to keep gossip at bay. When in public, she retained the polite aloof demeanor she usually assumed during the Season. Hart made certain ladies of the *ton* noted how gallant and attentive the duke was to his new duchess.

In private, Willa kept to herself, sometimes taking meals with Hart, but often dining alone in her rooms. Hart made himself scarce, confining himself to his study where work kept him busy, or visiting Brooks. The state of affairs with Willa grated on him, but he was determined to give his wife the wide berth she craved, despite his extreme frustration that he and Willa had not shared a bed since their wedding night.

About a week after their return, Hart made a decision he'd been grappling with since they'd learned the truth about Bellingham. He couldn't hold his wife hostage. He came to the realization that she would never belong to him unless she chose to.

Willa had accused Gus of keeping her in a cage for his own amusement. Guilt stung Hart. Was he now doing the same thing? It was a benign confinement to be sure, but Willa was a rare and beautiful bird who had grown weary of being in her cage. She needed to be set free. Anguish seared his chest. He alone could give Willa what she truly needed. Even if it meant giving up what mattered most to him.

• • •

Willa changed for bed and dismissed her maid, exhausted by the pretense she'd had to keep up in the weeks since returning from Fairview. A tap sounded on the other side of the door which adjoined Hart's rooms to hers. She jumped up from her dressing table, startled by the unexpected visit. Hart had not come to her rooms since their wedding night. Perhaps he'd decided to demand his husbandly rights. Her heart stumbled at the thought.

Hart let himself in. His angular features took on a harsh cast tonight and the expression on his face was one Willa could not quite interpret. He still wore his dark evening clothes, only his cravat was gone and his starched white shirt was open at the neck, revealing the dark hairs licking his throat.

He sat on the side of her bed. "I'm letting you go."

Willa froze. "What?"

"This is clearly a marriage you do not want. As much as I've wanted to deny it, we wouldn't be here if it were not for Bellingham's machinations. You'd likely have married or chosen a different course long ago."

After feeling emotionally numb for the past month, she was surprised to feel anxiety bubble up in her. "You are divorcing me?"

"I could keep you tied to me. Lord knows I want to." His tone was bleak. "I thought I could be happy just to have a small piece of you. But I can't. I'm too greedy. Each day I see the light in you diminish a little more."

All at once, Willa felt chilled. A barren sensation sliced straight through her bones. She moved to the fireplace, trying to draw its heat into her.

"If it's a divorce you want, I will give it to you. But a divorce would be a disaster for both of us," Hart said from behind her. "What I am proposing is an understanding that will all but give you your freedom. I will set you up in your own house. A portion of money has already been set aside to handle household expenses and staff. You also have your dowry. It will give you the independence you crave."

Willa tried to squelch the pang in her chest. She turned to face Hart, the heat from the hearth licking at her back. "And if I choose to bring another man into my bed?"

Hart winced. "I'm releasing you from our agreement in regards to outside affairs."

Willa examined Hart's face. "And you will seek comfort elsewhere?"

He exhaled, pushing to his feet, moving toward her like a man who carried a heavy burden. "I'm no saint, Willa. I would prefer to have you in my bed. Always." He smiled softly at the unruly curl that had fought its way out of Willa's nightcap. He moved the strand aside. "But if I can't have you, I will look for someone to give me warmth."

Jealousy shot up her spine. "And what of heirs?"

"It is up to you. I hope you will agree to share my bed often enough for us to have children. And after we have an heir, I won't expect you to come to my bed ever again." He placed the back of his hand against her cheek. "I release you. As completely as I can."

Pain paralyzed Willa's chest at the thought of losing him. "Is this what you want?"

He leaned in and brushed a kiss on her lips. The impact of it sparked through her, burning his touch into her memory. "It is what I desire for you. I want you to be happy. To be free to make your own choices." Hart pulled away and walked back to his chamber, closing the adjoining door on any hope of a true marriage.

Willa stood watching for the door for several minutes as the full meaning of Hart's words sank in. At long last, the freedom she'd craved was finally hers. So why did it feel as though someone had driven a blade into her heart?

• • •

Hart sat near the hearth in his chambers and took a swig of brandy. He closed his eyes, feeling the hard burn against his eyelids. He'd let her go. It had taken everything in him to release her, but part of him actually felt relieved.

He needed to move on. He would find an accommodating mistress. Not an actress or singer. He was done with that. Maybe a nice widow. Someone almost respectable with whom he could build a future, even if she couldn't be his wife. He'd seen many other men do it. Their wives were their duty—their mistresses the women they truly desired. They even had families with their amours. Provided nicely for them.

Lost in thought, he didn't hear the adjoining door open. He didn't notice Willa until she was almost in front of him, wearing a diaphanous white night rail he'd never seen before. Backlit by the fire, the gown left little to the imagination. He could see the clear outline of Willa's soft full breasts—punctuated by the awakened pearls at the center of them. She wore no nightcap, allowing her full curls to fall about her shoulders. A familiar rush of desire blasted to his groin.

She knelt down in front of him, between his legs, and her immense eyes glittered in the firelight. "You married me even though you thought I had given myself to another man. Tell me why."

Aching for her, he reached out to wrap a silken dark curl around his finger. "Because no woman compares to you."

"A man in your position can have anyone."

"I want you."

Her eyes glistened. "You have me." She began to pull off Hart's white linen shirt. His body reacted instantly. He inhaled in surprise, bringing his hands down over hers to stop their progress. "Willa—"

She pushed his hands aside and continued her efforts. The brush of her fingers against his skin made his body hungry and hard. "I'm here, Hart. Isn't this what you want?"

Hart's head screamed with a cross between joy and relief. "Are you certain?"

"It is the only thing I am sure of." She pulled off his shirt.

He lifted his arms to help her. Willa ran her fingers over the fuzz of hair on his chest. "I want you, Hart. Please take me to your bed."

The pleasure of her hands on him was almost unbearable. To his own amazement, Hart shook his head as he watched her touch him. "I cannot."

Her hands stilled. She looked up at him with pained eyes. "You no longer want me."

"I need to know what this is, Willa. Are you coming to me as part of the arrangement? To produce an heir?"

She shook her head. "I'm coming to you fully, as your wife. You gave me the freedom to choose and I choose you."

"But I thought you wanted to control you own destiny."

"Quite right. And I'm taking control by saying I want to be married to you by choice. Not because I was compromised into it. I know now that I love you and never want to be parted from you." Her hand began moving over him again, taking in the grooves of his chest and stomach. "I do not want to be released from our agreement. Nor will I release you. There will be no ladybirds for you, husband."

Hart's pulse began to pound in his head. Craving slammed through every inch of him.

"What I am saying is that I expect to satisfy you in every way," she said, repeating his words from that day at the pond. "So that you will never need to look elsewhere to sate your carnal urges." Her fingers moved to unfasten his breeches.

His arousal sprang free, hard and twitching. She stroked his length. He almost bucked out of his chair at her touch. Rising to his feet, he pulled her up with him. She was flushed, warm and alive in his arms. And she wanted him. Keeping her gaze locked on his, Willa stepped back and shyly removed her nightgown.

Hart's pulse howled at the gleaming perfection before him. The firelight danced over Willa's porcelain skin and soft full curves. Her cheeks shone pink and the tips of her breasts were pert with expectation. The sight of her made Hart's body unbearably hard. He reached out, his finger toying with the tips of her breasts.

She inhaled, passion infusing her face. "I expect you to satisfy me in every way." She took his hand, pulling Hart toward the bed. "I need you to sate my carnal urges."

His body roared in response. Tugging his breeches down, he stumbled toward the bed. "I can see you plan to be a very demanding wife." Grinning, he pulled her down onto the bed with him. They collapsed half-laughing with giddiness and hunger, their mouths reaching for each other.

But Hart was not about to be rushed. He indulged himself, going slowly, tasting and loving every part of her. He treated her body with reverence, touching and massaging her, kissing and licking. Hart was lost to his own abandon in a field of endless pleasure. When he finally brought his lips back to hers, Willa's mouth received him eagerly. His tongue was seeking, demanding, tasting the woman he had hungered for. They took each other wildly, need and craving scorching them in a delicious agony. When he could wait no longer, Hart positioned himself between her legs.

"Are you ready for me, Willa?" he whispered.

She smiled her acquiescence, but Hart saw the wrinkle of concern form between her eyebrows. He kissed it away. "I will be gentle, darling. I promise. I will never willingly hurt you again."

Her eyes glistened as she nodded and urged him toward

her. He nudged at her entrance and then slid into her in one smooth movement. She jerked with pleasure and moaned his name as he filled her.

He began to move within her, savoring her tightness, the satiny warmth, the unadulterated pleasure of finally being joined with her in the most elemental way. He moved over her, his strokes becoming deeper and more insistent. Determined that she would enjoy coupling this time, he reached down and touched her feminine flesh as he moved inside her, coaxing Willa into oblivion with him.

She stilled, then convulsed and trembled with a breathy sigh. Male satisfaction roared through him and he finally let himself go, allowing his body the explosive release it craved. Shaking violently, he cried out and buried his head in the crook of her soft neck. The final tremors of his release shook through him as he spilled his seed into her.

Afterwards, they lay still, clasping each other but not moving, save the rapid rise and fall of their chests. Still intimately connected, Hart closed his eyes and savored the aftertaste of their lovemaking, marveling at how his body hummed with sensation. How it already wanted more.

The feel of her body quivering beneath his pierced his revelry. Alarm arrowed through his heart. Was she weeping? He pulled back to look into her face, expecting to see tears, but instead discovered a face full of mirth.

"Tell me you aren't laughing," he said incredulously, still struggling to catch his breath. Her eyes glistened and her smile widened, her body shaking with merriment. It had been so long since he'd seen her truly amused, but this seemed like a deuced inappropriate time for laughter. Especially when he thought he'd performed admirably. "Laughter at a time such as this could seriously wound my manly pride."

"Oh no, never that." Her mouth quaked with amusement. "I was just thinking about how much time I've wasted brooding when we could have been doing this."

Satisfaction and relief loosened his tense limbs. "Ah, so you did not find my lovemaking technique to be lacking."

"Quite the contrary." She planted a hard kiss on his lips. "I may never let you leave my chamber."

Blood raced to his prick. "How convenient it is that I have no pressing engagements for the next few days."

"Then I suppose it is not too early to begin making up for wasted time." She wiggled her plush warm form suggestively beneath him. His languid blood began to rush faster. He toyed with the tip of one of her breasts, watching himself rub a gentle finger over it, his light strokes flattering it to reawaken.

Willa watched, her own fingers tightening as she raked them through his loose, long strands. "I love your hair this way, wild and free. You look so fierce."

"Do you plan to tame me?" His fingers left her breast and reached down between their joined bodies to the soft, wet place between her legs. Her breathing deepened and he sensed the primal urge begin to overtake her again.

"Goodness, I hope not," she said, bucking against his slickening fingers.

Hardening inside of her, he began to move in slow gentle movements, relishing her feminine place with his hands and prick, loving her mouth with his. Need and urgency overtook him and he thrust harder, faster, and deeper. Until he reached oblivion again with a shout of exhilaration and knew he'd found perfection in an imperfect world.

. . .

"Hart, what should we do about my private bank account now?" Willa popped a piece of cold chicken meat into her mouth. They were lounging on the bed they hadn't left for two days. Oblivious to time and structure, they'd made love countless times, sleeping only when overcome with delightful physical exhaustion.

He couldn't even be certain what day it was. Hart left the room only once, to tell his valet to cancel all appointments and invitations and to inform all callers that he and Willa were not at home to receive visitors.

He'd never slept so soundly. Last evening's erotic dream had seemed particularly vivid. Then he'd opened his eyes to the vision of Willa on top of him, riding him to awakening. She'd looked like a goddess, her tousled curls giving her the look of a well-bedded woman. Her full breasts swayed as she rode him, their pink nubs pert and reaching. He joined her in all eagerness, helping guide her hips until they both hurtled toward a frenzied rapture.

"So," Willa repeated, breaking through his memory of last night's wild ride, "what do you think?" She sat cross-legged, wearing one of his white shirts and nothing else. Hart lounged on his side across the tray of food from her. His chest was bare. Although he had pulled his breeches on, they remained unfastened.

Hart put a grape in his mouth. "I think you should take that shirt off. I want to see you."

Willa smiled, taking another bite of meat. "In all seriousness, there is no need for the bank account anymore.

I trust you. I don't desire anything in my name alone."

He ran admiring eyes over his wife. Her eyes sparkled with life and her cheeks flushed beautifully against the porcelain perfection of her skin. "I can't have a serious discussion with you until you take off that shirt."

Her eyebrows rose in amusement. "I'm still hungry." Licking her lips, she took another bite.

Hart's body stirred at the sight of Willa's pink tongue slipping along her full swollen mouth. "Then by all means, continue to eat." His blood simmered. "But I must insist you do it without a shirt. I want my shirt back. Post haste."

She reached for a small cake and he looked down her shirt when she did, the deep v-neck giving him an excellent view of the way her abundant, creamy breasts swayed when she moved. He reached out to cup her, but she swatted him away, snatching a cake and settling back out of his grasp.

"No, don't touch me until we have this discussion," she said firmly.

"What discussion was that?" he asked, mesmerized by the way her breasts jiggled beneath his shirt.

"My separate bank account." Her words barely registered through the fog of his mounting frustration. He reached for her again. But she was ready and deftly dodged him. "Come on, Hart, focus."

He tried to concentrate. "No, I think you should keep the funds in your own name. Although I will provide generously for you in the event of my death, I want you to have the dowry as well. You shall also have a generous allowance for your everyday expenses."

Willa popped a grape into her mouth. Hart watched her pink tongue slide out to lick its juice from her lips. "I suppose that makes sense," she said, considering his words. "May I do as I wish with my dowry?"

"Yes, do what you please with it." He ran his hand over the smooth silk of her bare thigh. "If you won't let me touch you, then I insist that you touch yourself. It's only fair."

"What?" He'd finally distracted her attention away from her bank account. "Why would I do that?" she asked, a slight frown of confusion on her face.

"Because it excites me."

Willa blushed hotly, her eyes widening. "Truly?"

He smiled. "I'm relieved to see you thinking about something other than food and money. I was beginning to worry."

"How would I touch myself?" she asked with an almost clinical curiosity.

"The way I would touch you," he said, his gaze moving hungrily over her body.

She misinterpreted the look in his eyes. "Aren't you hungry? You've barely eaten."

"Quite right," he said, finally losing all restraint. He pulled her shirt off and flipped her over on her back in one fluid movement. Hart grabbed the sweet cream from the tray before completely overturning it as he moved atop her.

"What are you doing?" He answered by spreading the cream all over her, rubbing it over her breasts and the softly rounded slope of her belly and to other scandalous hard-to-reach places.

"Suddenly, I'm starved," he said, licking his way down her belly. Hart took his time, partaking fully in the sumptuous banquet of her body while she moaned and writhed beneath him.

And he did not stop until his hunger was completely satisfied.

• • •

"What the devil is taking so bloody long?" Hart demanded of the short, sturdy man in spectacles sitting across the desk in his study.

"It seems, Your Grace, that someone of standing, other than yourself, of course, is purchasing the Earl of Bellingham's debts," said his solicitor, James Ogden.

A few weeks prior, Hart had hatched a plan to acquire all of Bellingham's vowels. The purpose was simple: buy up all of the debt and ruin the whoreson for what he'd done to Willa. He'd easily acquired sixty percent of Bellingham's IOUs before running into this barrier.

"Who is it?" he barked. "Who is getting in my way?"

"The buyer apparently wishes to remain anonymous."

"How much has he acquired?"

"About forty percent of the earl's gaming debt."

"So Bellingham has other enemies who want to own him. I wonder for what purpose." Hart sat back in his chair with his interlaced hands on his chest. "Whatever his reasons, I want those vowels. Find this person and buy him out."

Ogden cleared his throat. "I have been in touch with his representative. He is willing to sell."

"Excellent."

"At triple their value."

"Triple? That's highway robbery!" He rose and went to look out the window to calm himself down. As a businessman, he was used to having the upper hand. That included having the luxury to walk away from a bad deal. He couldn't shake the uneasy feeling that the seller seemed to know how badly he wanted the vowels.

Ogden did not react to Hart's angry outburst. He remained impassive, rising from his chair across from the massive desk in Hart's study. "Your Grace, I'm afraid the seller has another demand."

Hart turned from the window to look at Ogden. "Dare he suggest he requires more than triple the value of the vowels?"

"He insists you meet him in person to transact the deal."

"Whatever for?"

"I'm not certain, Your Grace. He asks that you meet this afternoon at Green's, the new hotel on Albemarle Street. Suite 102."

A few hours later, Hart made his way to the first fine hotel to open in Mayfair. Composed of several townhouses, Green's offered luxury suites to its most exclusive clientele. Stepping into one of them, he closed the door behind him and surveyed the well-appointed parlor, anxious to meet the bastard who was trying to fleece him.

"At last we meet," said a warm, feminine voice.

Chapter Fifteen

Hart knew that voice. He heard it in his dreams—the robust sound of warm, dark chocolate. He turned to find Willa standing in the doorway that led to the bed chamber, a knowing smile on her face.

"What the devil?" said Hart. "What are you doing here?"

"You've come to meet the person who holds forty percent of Augustus' vowels."

"Yes, but—" He halted, raising his brows in disbelief. "You? But how?"

Willa settled on the parlor's burgundy velvet sofa. "You told me to use my dowry as I saw fit."

"You are the person who's been buying up Bellingham's vowels?" he asked incredulously.

She smiled at the surprise she saw in his face. "I hired someone Cam recommended to acquire them for me, using the funds from my dowry."

Hart dropped down by her side, grudging admiration

gradually replacing his exasperation. "So you bid up the price. You've cost me a fortune."

"In my defense, I was not aware that you were the other buyer until you agreed to pay my astronomical asking price. No one else would go to those lengths." She looked at him with dancing eyes. "Really, Hart, I thought you prided yourself in being an unparalleled businessman."

Hart let out a gruff laugh. "You minx. That is why I sensed the seller knew how much I wanted those bloody vowels."

Willa slipped her hand into his. "No one would know better than I."

"Well, a deal is a deal. You shall have your coin and I will own all of Bellingham's vowels."

Willa gave him a wary look. "What are you going to do with them?"

Hart grinned, the humor in the situation not lost on him. "In truth, I was going to gift them to you once I had acquired all of them. But at this moment, I'm considering changing my mind."

"Oh, Hart." Her eyes shined. "What a lovely thing to do. You planned to give them to me to do whatever I chose?"

"Very lovely for you. You've managed to both triple your money and acquire the vowels." He stood up, pulling her along with him toward the bedchamber.

"What now?" Willa asked, willingly following him.

"Now," he said. "I am going to allow you to show me just how much you appreciate my very generous gift."

• • •

She showed him in every way she could imagine. Two hours later, their exhausted glistening bodies were intertwined in the massive bed. Willa's head lay on Hart's chest while she toyed with the smattering of tight dark curls there.

Hart gave a lazy smile. "I must say, you certainly have an excellent way of showing your appreciation." He yawned, looking very pleased with himself. "I must arrange gifts for you much more often."

Laughing, she placed a light kiss on his chest. "What shall I do with the vowels?"

"Why were you purchasing them? Surely you had a plan. Something to give Gus his comeuppance?"

"I did have revenge in mind when I began purchasing the debt." She sighed, her soft curves snuggling into his warm body. "But now…honestly, I was thinking about selling all of the vowels even before I realized you were the anonymous buyer."

"Why would you do that?"

"Once I realized the enormity of Augustus' debt, I comprehended that I didn't have the means to buy all of it." She adjusted her body slightly so she could look at Hart. As she did so, she savored the supple warmth of bare skin upon bare skin. "I want you to buy me out."

"I've already given you all of the vowels."

"Yes, and now I'd like you to buy them back. I have better uses for the funds."

He guffawed, the sound rumbling deep in his chest. "Indeed? So let me be clear about this. I've already gifted you the debt, which you made me pay triple the value for. Now you want me to *buy* back the gift I've just paid a fortune for?"

She smiled, her mind already working furiously on her new plan. "Exactly."

"Why do I have the feeling you plan to drive a hard bargain?"

"I will, of course, demand top coin for it."

"To what end?" He ran his fingers over the smooth white curve of her shoulder. "Will you drive me to ruin just for sport?"

"I want to open more coffee houses for women and street children. We could open one in Bath."

"With your special teas?"

The idea of having a worthy project of her own—one that could keep more women and children off the streets—left her giddy with excitement. "Of course. What do you think?"

His large, warm hands rubbed her bare shoulders. "I think it's an excellent idea."

"Truly?"

He kissed her hard. "Truly."

"And I shall expect a very good price for the sugar you supply to the coffee houses."

"I am to be your new supplier as well?" He lifted a dark brow. "I expect to be properly compensated."

She returned his demanding kiss. "I begin to comprehend what sort of payment you have in mind."

"What about Gus?"

She yawned and stretched over him. "I could care less what happens to Augustus. I want him out of my life and my thoughts. Revenge takes energy and I don't want to expend anything on him."

Hart's hands slipped off her shoulders and under the

counterpane, kneading her upper back as she lay atop him, stomach to stomach, chest to chest. "Then leave it all to me."

"Mmmm, that's nice." Willa closed her eyes, enjoying his touch. "He's already all but ruined himself, you know."

His hands stilled. "Gus?"

She wriggled her shoulders under his motionless hands. "Don't stop." When he picked back up again, she continued with a satisfied sigh. "Do you know the Bellingham country seat is no longer entailed? The earl allowed the tail to lapse. Possibly to give himself the flexibility to sell off parts of the estate. That would leave Race and Addie without a home."

"But surely her dowry is as generous as yours." Hart's hands worked their way lower, to the curve of her lower back. "They could still live quite comfortably."

"Yes, but Race refuses to make use of it."

"How honorable." His long, warm fingers slid over the curves of her bottom, cupping and squeezing. "Quite a different sort than his brother."

Desire tugged deep in her belly. "The two are unalike in every way. Race is decent to the core. He has a true connection to the land. Addie fears Race will be crushed if Bellingham Park and the surrounding estate pass out of the family."

She reached up to kiss his lips. It was sweet, soft, and fleeting. After an exhausting afternoon of lovemaking, it surprised her to feel Hart thickening again against her thigh.

"Well, I have not lost my taste for revenge." His fingers kneaded her bottom with a more insistent touch. "What would you say if I told you I have a plan to deal with Gus which would also protect your sister?"

She gave him a hot, lingering kiss. "I should be most

appreciative."

He lifted Willa by the waist, bringing her down on his engorged flesh. She sat astride him, pushing down until he was fully sheathed. Cupping her breasts in his large hands, Hart began to move indolently beneath her.

"Come now, darling, show me just how grateful you would be."

. . .

Augustus Manning was in a hurry. He barely gave his coachman time to stop before alighting from the carriage and bounding into Green's Hotel. He demanded to be directed to the suite, arriving at the appointed destination to find the door had been left ajar. Augustus' arousal ached with anticipation. Willa awaited him in this suite. He shoved the door open only to find the opulent sitting room empty. He looked around with urgent desire, barely able to endure any longer. His sweeping gaze found the entrance to the bed chamber.

Perhaps she was already abed waiting for him. Willa's note had asked Augustus to meet her here at this time. She had come to her senses, it seemed. He imagined her stripped of all her clothes, begging for forgiveness.

He ought not to forgive her for denying him the right of taking her maidenhead. Still, cuckolding Hartwell would be equally satisfying. Perhaps even more so. And he felt certain Willa was the woman who could bring out the man in him again. He had trouble staying hard with other women, unless the interaction involved a bit of rough play. But that was only because they were all whores. It would be different with

Willa.

He thought of the things he would do to her. He would punish her and then he would take her. He would use every part of her over and over again until she begged for mercy. His arousal agitating him beyond measure, Augustus burst into the hotel bed chamber looking wildly around for Willa. The bed clothes had already been disturbed. But a quick look revealed Willa wasn't among them.

His blood iced when he spotted the dark-clad figure in a comfortable chair by the bed. "Hartwell."

"You were expecting someone else?" Clad in all black, the duke's dark hair was tied back in that ridiculous queue he favored. It emphasized his harsh features, the strong nose and sharp cheekbones. Augustus suppressed a shiver. The man looked like the devil.

His stomach dropped. "What in bloody hell?"

Blue black eyes regarded him with cold clarity. "You were expecting my wife perhaps?" Hartwell lit a cheroot and exhaled, infusing the air with the smell of burning tobacco. "Are you here for an assignation?" Hartwell made a careless gesture toward the rumpled bed clothes. "As you can see, you are too late. My wife was just here. Unlike you, I don't bring women to private chambers unless I am confident of the outcome. But to be honest, it was my wife who rented the room and lured me here. You can imagine my surprise… and delight."

A shudder of disgust rippled through Augustus at the thought of the scoundrel's hands on Willa. "Your wife invited me here. It seems you don't have what it takes to satisfy her."

Hartwell took a drag off his cheroot and watched as he exhaled small tight circles of pearly smoke. "Oh, believe me, satisfaction has never been a problem."

Augustus' insides curled with hatred. "I fondly recall another rented room much like this one some four years ago. I am very well aware of the pleasures she offers."

"Spare me." Swarthy skin stretched taut over the devil's uncompromising features. "We both know you have no intimate knowledge of her pleasures. As her husband, I am in a unique position to know. However, I am not here to discuss my wife."

"Why are we here?" Augustus suppressed the urge to spit on the demon's polished boots. "Do get on with it. I haven't got all day."

An icy smile. "Off to place a bet somewhere?"

"That's none of your concern."

Another frosty turn of the devil's mouth. "I'm delighted to inform you that it is indeed my concern. Do you know that there are enough vowels out there to ruin you?" Hartwell's eyes were intent on his cheroot as he took another slow drawn-out drag. Followed by tightly controlled small white circles. The silence screamed in Augustus' ears.

Hartwell crossed his legs, his gleaming black Hessians catching the light. "Owing little bits of coin to many different parties is manageable, provided you are adept at juggling." Hartwell's gaze reached Augustus' eyes. "But can you imagine what could happen if all of those vowels were in the hands of one person?"

A wintry blast slammed through Augustus, depriving him of air. He sank down on the padded bench at the foot the bed, wondering for the first time just how much he really owed. He never bothered to pay attention. Surely it couldn't be that bad.

"Unlike you, I mind the numbers," said Hartwell. "I examine them in very close detail. Close enough to know you are ruined."

"Like hell, you say." Nausea swirled in Augustus' gut. "I'll sell Bellingham Park, the entire estate, to settle this debt. You don't own me, Hartwell."

"That might be an agreeable plan," Hartwell said, his mouth curving upward into a chilling smile, "if you had not already bet away Bellingham Park."

Augustus blanched. How could Hartwell already know about the note on Bellingham Park? That had happened at White's just a few days ago. He intended to win the family estate back right away.

"Yes, I hold the vowels on Bellingham Park," Hartwell said, answering the unasked question. "And your London town house alone won't settle your debts. I'll have you in debtor's prison within a fortnight. You will be completely ruined."

Augustus' legs quivered. He barked a harsh laugh, longing to slice that smug look off the demon's face. "I will marry an heiress, a wealthy one. That will cover my debts."

Hartwell raised a brow. "And will you tell her that you are unmanned? That you cannot sire children?"

Augustus' chest felt as though an enormous stallion was bucking against it. He could barely take air into his desperate lungs. "What are you talking about?"

"Your mistresses are very accommodating, especially when coin is involved. Although some of them were willing to sell you out for a tumble. But we both know I am a very happily married man so that was of no interest."

Augustus' temper flared. "You, sir, are disgusting and

unworthy of her—"

Hartwell continued as though Augustus had not spoken. "I was very interested to hear there are doubts about your virility among the lightskirts you associate with. So I had my man investigate further." Hart paused, taking a luxurious pull of his cheroot. "It is interesting that you are unable to complete the act with a woman unless, not surprisingly, it involves violence or some sort of depravity. I understand your whores have to use their considerable skills to keep your rod at attention. The equipment seems to work all right until you actually try to bed a woman in the traditional way."

Augustus emitted a laugh of genuine amusement. "You always were a fool who never understood the true power of the peerage. There will always be an heiress willing to wed an earl, no matter how low on funds or hapless he may be."

"Perhaps. But an heiress with the amount of blunt you need can afford to be choosy. Why would she take a risk on someone such as yourself?"

He relaxed, feeling the power shift in the room. "I shall make some plain nobody a countess. Surely, even you are not so addle-brained that you can't comprehend the power of that."

"I will personally see to it that your malady is well known. Imagine the tales the *ton* will tell about the limp earl's hapless attempts to catch an unsuspecting heiress."

Augustus sat forward, his elbows resting on his thighs. "People like us are never held to account. You should know that better than anyone." His eyes held Hart's. "Just ask Erskine."

"The man you raped."

"It was all in good fun." Augustus smiled at the memory,

recalling the rush of excitement he'd felt during the incident. "He was lucky to be among his betters."

"I doubt that was his thinking when you and your friends held him down and took turns violating him."

"He fought like the devil, I can tell you that." His blood heated at the memory of the vicar's son struggling as they mounted him, one after the other. But the skinny bastard had refused to give them the satisfaction of hearing him scream. He hadn't uttered a sound as each rowdy drunkard had extracted his pleasure from Erskine's unwilling body. "But his sort never win, it is the way of the world."

"You are no longer dealing with the son of a vicar." Disgust twisted Hartwell's features. "You cannot harm people without regard for the consequences. You will not escape so easily this time."

"You are so wrong. I already have." Augustus savored the cool satisfaction of victory that settled deep in his bones. "I've had both a duke and the daughter of a marquess attacked, all without consequence."

The devil stiffened. "You are responsible for Willa's attack at the coffee house?"

"I arranged much more than that. I made certain her tea delivery went missing to see if she would try to replace it. I wanted her good and frightened so she would give up such silliness." To Augustus' supreme satisfaction, Hartwell's fingers whitened as they gripped the arms of his chair.

"How could you know she would be in the alley that afternoon?"

"She was riding in my carriage and, like a fool, alighted to continue the rest of the journey on foot. I sent my footman after her to impart a lesson she wouldn't soon forget." He smiled. "The scheme was brilliant until you stepped in and ruined my plans. Setting footpads upon you seemed the most expedient way to be rid of your tiresome presence."

"You hired the footpads who attacked me outside of Brooks," he said in an even voice. "What was their mission exactly?"

"To knife you in the gut and leave you for dead," he snarled, allowing the full depth of his hatred to saturate his voice. "Clearly, they botched the mission."

"Clearly." Hartwell took a leisurely drag on his cheroot. "Why are you so certain I won't have you hanged for what you've done?"

"Who will believe you? Everyone knows you've hated me since university."

"I thrashed you after coming upon you leading the attack on Erskine."

"But no one knows that."

"I gave Erskine my word of honor that I would never breathe a word of it to anyone."

Augustus smiled. "Interesting how that has worked to my advantage. They all think you harbor a deep-seated jealousy of me. If you bring these baseless claims before the lords, they shall laugh you out of the chamber."

"Tell me, Gus" —cold dark eyes assessed him— "do you ever wonder what became of Erskine?"

"Never. Why would I?"

"Because he rose to become a magistrate here in London."

Augustus brows lifted. "I suppose that is as high as a vicar's son can expect to reach. I fail to see what interest that would be to me."

A voice came from the doorway. "It is of interest because I have just heard your confession." Erskine stood on the threshold. No longer a thin, slight boy, this man carried himself with confident certainty. "You've just admitted to attempting to murder a duke and to attacking the daughter of a marquess."

Augustus' stomach heaved.

The devil smiled. "I see you begin to comprehend. Both a duke and a magistrate have heard your confession."

The contents of Augustus' stomach spiraled upward with stunning speed. Unable to stop the bile-fueled surge, he wretched, spewing vomit across the floor. Humiliation coursed through him at the sight of disgorged matter splattered on his boots.

Hartwell gave a small snort of disgust. "So here is what will happen. You will go abroad at once. I don't care where to. You will never show your spineless face in England again."

Erskine shot Augustus an expressionless glance before turning to go. "Your Grace, if that is all, I have matters to attend to. My men are outside if you have need of them."

Hartwell nodded. "Thank you for coming."

Perspiration clouded Augustus' vision. He pushed to his feet, trying not to sway. Sidestepping the mess on the floor to move away from Hart, he uttered, "This is ludicrous."

"Consider yourself fortunate. I spare you a trial by your peers so that my wife's sister won't be tainted by your disgrace."

The walls closed in on him, the sound of his own breathing screamed in his ears. "You will not get away with this."

"I already have. Pray control yourself, Gus. I'm in

a hurry to go home to my duchess. Now listen and listen well. You will go abroad. I will retain the vowels. Your brother, Horace, and my lovely new sister, Adela, will run the earldom in your absence. I understand Horace is quite good with numbers." Hartwell paused to brush lint off of his jacket. "The terms of my conditions are that you never marry, which alleviates the very slight risk that you might actually be capable of begetting a legitimate heir. Adela and Horace's son will inherit. Until then, I shall be content to let Horace make reasonable payments from estate rents and profits. And who knows, perhaps my wife and I will forgive the remaining debt once our nephew inherits your title."

Panic fogged Augustus' mind. He couldn't let this man ruin him. To go abroad, he would be reduced to nothing. The humiliation of it was too much to bear. His gut wrenched again but his stomach was already empty. "And if I refuse?"

Hart sauntered over to the dresser, crushing his cheroot down into a plate to extinguish it. "I will use all of my considerable power as the Duke of Hartwell to see you tried and hanged for attempting my murder. Our peers will not look kindly upon someone who tried to do away with one of their own."

His stomach turned over again, making his mouth water with the sour taste of bile. "I'll see you in Hades."

"Just as long as I never see you in England again." The demon's dagger-like features sharpened. He approached and brought his mouth close to Augustus' ear. "No estate. No fortune. No heir. Your unfortunate line ends here. I have all but obliterated you."

Murderous hatred and despair raged through Augustus. He was helpless to control his destiny. His legs began to give way, so he sank down onto the bed.

"Interesting, isn't it, that you plotted my wife's demise in a chamber much like this one. But it is your ruin that has been orchestrated here today." Hartwell strode from the room and paused in the doorway, his face dark with satisfaction.

"You are ruined. Utterly and completely."

· · ·

Willa sat at her dressing table regarding herself in the mirror. She was dressed for the ball her mother and Cam were throwing at Camryn House. She wore the silver and lace gown from her wedding and her hair was dressed in a similar fashion, with light touches of silver interwoven among her curls.

She was so focused on studying her reflection she didn't notice Hart come in until he stood behind her. He, too, had already dressed for the ball in his usual stark black formal wear with a blinding white cravat, his hair pulled back.

"Admiring your beauty, I see." He looked at her in the mirror. "Not that I blame you. I can barely take my eyes off of you myself." He cupped her cheek tenderly with his hand.

Willa's heart leapt as she looked at her husband. His confident bearing and sharp dark features never failed to light a little fire inside her. Willa's eyes returned to her own reflection. "Am I really beautiful? Both Flor and Addie say it is so. Can you credit it?"

Hart smiled and dropped a kiss at the nape of Willa's neck, the sensual warmth of his lips causing her to shudder with pleasure. "Of course I believe that. Everyone knows you are beautiful, Willa." His hand rested on her shoulder. "Everyone but you apparently."

Willa put her hand over Hart's where it rested on her shoulder. "How is it possible to be beautiful and not be aware of it?"

Hart gave her shoulder a reassuring squeeze. "Bellingham made certain gentlemen stayed away from you. You weren't courted as you should have been given that you are a diamond of the first water."

She felt a pang of anger. "A piece of my self-regard. Another thing he stole from me." Her eyes caught Hart's in the mirror. "Speaking of Augustus, I hear he has gone abroad. Do you know anything about that?" Hart shrugged, allowing his hand to drift from Willa's shoulder deep into her décolletage.

She closed her eyes, heat chasing through her. Standing, she turned around to face Hart with a luminous smile. "I suppose I should thank him. Augustus Manning brought me the greatest gift of all."

Hart furrowed his brow, his blue-black eyes darkening. "And what exactly might that be?"

She reached up to kiss him. "You, of course, foolish man. If he hadn't interfered with my life, I might have married some boring viscount long before you decided to come back from India. That would have been a true tragedy."

"Speaking of India." He took her into his arms. "I must undertake a voyage there in the near future to attend to business."

Her heart dropped. "How long will you be gone?"

"About three months. Do you think that will be enough time for me to show you India?"

She blinked. "Truly?"

"You said you wanted to see the world." His dark eyes sparkled. "We'll begin with the Taj Mahal. Perhaps we shall explore Greece next year."

She made an exclamation of surprise and threw her arms around him, sprinkling his face with kisses. "You are the finest husband any woman could ask for."

"It is admittedly a bit selfish on my part." His arms closed around her. "I cannot be without my duchess. And I am quite fond of the manner in which you choose to show your gratitude." He brought his lips down on hers with a fullness and urgency that startled Willa and began walking her backwards towards the bed.

"Hart," she laughed, breathless, trying to break free. "What are you doing? We are already dressed for Mother's ball."

He didn't seem to hear her. Hart swooped down, picking Willa up and tumbling onto the bed with her. His kisses were hungry and demanding. He tore away his cravat then reached to pull up the skirt of her silvery white dress.

Willa's body burned for him and she cried out when her husband's determined fingers reached the spot he'd been searching for. She tugged at Hart's shirt, trying to pull it off. "What are we doing? This is madness," she panted just before his mouth closed over hers again. He began to pull off her dress.

"Since you are in your wedding gown, I think it only appropriate that we replay our wedding night." Hart undid Willa's stays and slipped off her chemise, leaving his wife clad only in her stockings. "It did not end as satisfactorily as it should have."

His tongue began a tantalizing journey down her body. "And this time, dear wife, I promise to satisfy your every desire, since you have already delivered so thoroughly on all of mine."

Acknowledgments

As an author who benefits greatly from the expertise of her editors, I am fortunate to work with the outstanding team at Entangled Publishing. My sincere thanks go to Kate Fall, Alethea Spiridon Hopson, and Gwen Hayes, who gave me the best editing comment ever. And also to Rima Jean, who I was remiss in not thanking for her guidance on *Tempting Bella*.

My deepest gratitude goes to my fellow femmes, at The Violet Femmes blog, for always having my back, and to Faith Lapidus, for her unerring eye in helping spot errors before my books reach readers.

Speaking of readers, I want to thank everyone who has embraced my books. Hearing from you is one of the great pleasures of being an author!

About the Author

Diana Quincy is an award-winning former television journalist who decided she'd rather make up stories where a happy ending is always guaranteed.

Her books revolve around the Regency world of dashing dukes, irresistible rogues, and the headstrong women who capture their hearts. *New York Times* bestselling author Grace Burrowes called Diana's debut novel, *Seducing Charlotte*, "Sweet, steamy, and thoroughly enjoyable."

Growing up as a foreign-service brat, Diana lived in many countries and is now settled in Virginia with her husband and two sons. When not bent over her laptop or trying to keep up with laundry, she enjoys reading and spending time with her family, and dreams of traveling much more than her current schedule (and budget) allows.

Diana loves to hear from readers. You can keep up with her on Twitter, Facebook, and by visiting her website.

SEDUCING CHARLOTTE
Diana Quincy

Opposites attract…

Even if he is the catch of the season, Charlotte Livingston has a low opinion of the wildly handsome Marquess of Camryn. He's an industrialist who thinks nothing of replacing workers with machines, depriving them of honest work. Camryn is everything a social reformer like Charlotte detests. Besides, her loyalty belongs to another man.

Worlds collide…

As a violent rebellion rages across England, an undeniable attraction flares between the passionate adversaries. Camryn vows to destroy the rebel movement, unaware that the spinster who has captured his heart harbors a secret — a shocking connection to one of its leaders that could shatter them both.

Tempting Bella
Diana Quincy

"The Saint" has returned for his andaoned bride...

England 1810

Mirabella can hardly remember the man she married as a girl to settle a gaming debt between their fathers. And it's just as well. She feels nothing but contempt for the man who wed her for her fortune and promptly forgot she existed. The *ton* may call him "The Saint" but Bella knows better.

Forced to marry as a teen to rescue his family from certain ruine, Sebastian has been apart from his child bride since their wedding day. When he encounters an enchanting impish beauty at the opera, he's thrilled to find she is none other than his long-ago bride and he is more than ready to make her his wife in truth.

Too bad the beguilling beauty has no intention of coming meekly to the marriage bed.

CONFESSIONS OF LOVE
Melissa Blue

She can't trust her treacherous heart...

London, 1817

Lieutenant Jonathan Rycroft is intoxicating. His hands know just where to touch her, his lips know just how to trip her pulse, and his body knows just how to bring about every forbidden desire Lindsay Dunsfield has ever felt. He's the one man that's owned her heart…and he shattered it two years ago.

Returned to London on assignment with the War Office, Jonathan's mission is hindered by a love he cannot forget. One scorching kiss reignites the flames of their passion, but he inadvertently drags Lindsay into a mire of murder and deception that hits closer to home than she ever would have dreamed.

In a world where Lindsay can trust no one, will she find renewed faith in the last place she expected to look?

A VERY SCANDALOUS HOLIDAY ANTHOLOGY

Nancy Fraser, Sophia Garrett, Amber Lin, and
Crista McHugh

Four very spirited vignettes from holidays past...

Erin's Gift by Nancy Fraser
Chicago 1920s

Widower Seth Harrison has no intention of falling in love again but will he be able to resist the sweetness of his son's nanny, Erin O'Mara—his sister's best friend?

An Eternity of You by Sophia Garrett
England 1833

The Duke of Sharrington left Rebecca with more than a broken heart six years ago—he left her with a son. He's rekindled their passion with his return, but it will take a Christmas miracle to earn her heart.

Letters at Christmas by Amber Lin
England, late Regency

After three years at sea, Captain Hale Prescott has the means to marry the love of his life and his best friend's sister. Sidony Harbeck, however, might never speak to him again. Despite their whispered adolescent promises, he never wrote her a single letter...at least, none he ever sent.

Eight Tiny Flames by Crista McHugh
1944 Ardennes, WWII

Lt. Ruth Mencher has always secretly admired Capt. Joseph Klein, but it takes the lighting of a Hanukkah candle to uncover the spark of mutual attraction. Each night awakens a new facet of their relationship, but as the Battle of the Bulge begins, the approaching Nazi forces threaten to tear them apart.

THE HIGHWAYMAN'S BRIDE
Jane Beckenham

He's stolen her most valuable posession... her heart...

England, 1813

Forced into a marriage...

Compelled by her uncle to marry a man who has a predilection for violence, Tess Stanhope resorts to a ploy from her favorite novels to fund an escape - highwayman robbery. But her attempt is botched by a maddening, handsome rogue named Aiden.

Driven by revenge...

Aiden Masters, Lord of Charnley, is hell-bent on avenging his sister's brutal treatment at the hands of the criminal Florian Nash. He single-mindedly seeks vengeance at the expense of all else - even by furtively roaming the highways at night.

Blackmailed for love...

At a London party Tess meets up with Aiden once again and blackmails... marry her or she'll divulge to society has clandestine life as a highwayman. She desires a marriage in name only - but the more time they spend fighting their desire, the closer they come to giving in.

We hope you enjoyed your Scandalous read.
We have more where that came from!

Our readers know that historical doesn't mean antiquated. Scandalous romances are bold and sexy and passionate. After all, torrid love affairs are even more illicit when forbidden by social mores. Take a little time for yourself, escape to another era, and discover a timeless romance. There's never been a better time to fall in love.

Printed in Great Britain
by Amazon

81478753R00144